# My First Murder
by
Mark Flanagan
The Man That Loves You

ISBN:978-1-365-76426-4

## Dedication

This book is dedicated to all of my friends, and to all of my enemies.
It is also dedicated to all that I Love or have Loved.
And to all that Love or did Love me.
The book is also dedicated to all of the souls who touched my life and heart when they were with me on this plane and who will welcome my soul when I join them in their new existence.
Finally the book is dedicated to
my memories of the
Future.

When I wrote my first book my friend Robyn Holbert a.k.a. Annie Harrison, an accomplished author, told me to write about something I knew. All I knew about then was sex so I wrote "Episodes of A Male Slut." Which is available on Kindle. Unfortunately I know about something else now.

This book is about my new knowledge. Murder.

## Chapter 1 Decisions Decisions

Dark thoughts dimmed the bright sunny day as surely as if the blue sky was covered in rain clouds. I was walking through a neighborhood known locally as “Mortgage Hill”.

This is the part of town where the rich or the rich wanna-be’s built homes that were priced in the stratosphere as far as I was concerned.

There were cars in the driveways that cost enough money to send my kid to college.

These people probably worried about what brand of caviar to serve, while I am worried about how I can buy bread and beans for my family. How did my life come to this I wondered?

I am told that a little knowledge is a dangerous thing.

It is time now to understand that a little information can not only be a dangerous thing, but it can also be down right disastrous!

I finally understand how my life has come to this.

I can’t believe I hadn’t seen it before. Now, walking through this neighborhood trying to find work doing anything, my brain shifted from neutral to drive. I considered these facts; a lot of what the mines paid us was in script, which could only be spent in company stores.

We lived in rented company store shacks, bought company store furniture, and we ate company store groceries.

In essence we gave the company back a lot of our pay. We were doing dangerous life-threatening work for very little actual cash.

Not only did we make the owners filthy rich, we paid those bastards for the privilege of doing it. That's how my life had come to this!

My wife, Nora, and my child, Matthew, were at home counting on me to do what husbands and fathers are supposed to do. Be the provider.
I did just that when the coalmines were open.

My job in a low roof coalmine paid fifty dollars a day as a hand loader.
Our family didn't have a lot.

As I said, we lived in a coal camp shack, which was Company owned.
They charged us most of our script each month for a dump that was built of old boards, with tarpaper roofs.

There were vertical cracks in the walls so wide you could piss through them. Cold as hell in the winter but those cracks did give us a little relief on hot summer days.

We cooked our meals on a coal-burning cook stove.

In the winter we kept warm with a pot bellied, coal burning, heating stove.

There was no in-door plumbing.
The place was equipped with a hand pump for water from a well, plus a big wooden barrel just outside of the kitchen door acting as a cistern to catch rainwater.

We used a large steel washtub that doubled for clothes washing, and as a bathtub. The toilet was an outhouse. For those of you who do not know what an outhouse is here is a description of the place we used to eliminate our bodily waste.

An outhouse is a wooden shack built over a trench in the backyard. The place could normally only accommodate two persons.

The only furniture was a wooden bench with two holes cut in it to sit on.

As an extra luxury some of these hand-built comfort stations even had a tin can attached to a piece of old garden hose. The hose ran through a hole in the wooden floor, for the times when you didn't need to sit down.

There would also be a year-old catalog or some newspapers or, if you were lucky, maybe even a roll of toilet paper on the bench.

Not much of a life for you maybe but we were O.K. with it.

We grew up in that same environment.

I worked hard for eight hours a day, six days a week in a "room" I couldn't stand up in. My workspace was a hole in the side of a hole in the side of a West Virginia mountain. The roof of my room was so low I worked on my knees; shoveling up the kind of coal we called "bug dust".

It was the same kind of work my Dad did, until he died at forty-nine.

The paycheck came each week though, so we never really suffered. We even managed to stuff a few bucks in the old sock.

Thank goodness for our small nest egg. That pittance fed us and paid the rent while I looked for work.

I started my search for some kind of employment three months ago and I'm still on the hunt.

I haven't been out of a job for ninety days because I'm picky. I'll take anything that pays enough to feed the family.

My problem is simple. When Dad died it became my responsibility to support my Mother and younger brother, Jack.

I had to quit school in the eighth grade and start mining.

Well, you know the world keeps turning, things keep keepin' on.

Mom joined Dad, Jack got a job driving for Falls City Beer and got his own place; I was earning enough to take a wife, so Nora married me.

A grade school education or the ability to shoot a coal seam didn't qualify me for much of a job, other than shoveling bug dust and loading it into an open rail car. Hard as it is, I began to long for that old job back.

## Chapter 2 Pounding the Pavement

Also I wanted to kill my congressman for voting to expand the use of "clean energy".

Didn't that son of a bitch know they were doing a hell of a lot more damage with all this fucking fracking for natural gas? Plus some of us think cracking that shale is ruining our wells.

They were polluting the water in our mountain streams and lakes, killing the fish with the damned turbines.

Their shitty windmills are knocking birds right out of the sky.

Solar panels, that cost more than the electricity they produce, are occupying valuable land that might be used for food production.

Could we grow enough food to feed the world with those acres? There are those that say we could.

The scientists were throwing away an almost endless supply of usable energy that could be made as clean as a baby's fresh wiped ass.

Plus political votes were costing thousands of jobs, including mine, and causing me great mental and emotional anguish. Yes sir, they're doing a lot more harm than we did by simply digging for coal.

Don't get me wrong; I think we <u>do</u> need clean energy for some things. I <u>know</u> we need coal for a lot of things too.

I'm pretty damned sure that one of those brilliant cocksuckers could figure out a way to use all kinds of energy.

Another one of 'em could figure out what it takes to make the coal burn as clean as fresh air.

I'm really pissed! Can you tell?

It isn't fair that some have so much while we have so little. Actually we have next to nothing now, since J.D. closed the mine.

I know the Happytown mines were still making piles of money when J.D. Cooper, the mines owner, shut the operation down and kicked us out.

His coalmine just wasn't making enough moolah to satisfy the greedy millionaire asshole.

Mortgage Hill was probably filled with his same kind. People that exploited folks like me. How else could they afford these fancy wheels and sumptuous digs?

Miners like me, or other poor saps, must have worked their asses off to make the money these bloodsuckers took to the bank.

It's just not fair, that's all there is to it.

The Hoity-Toity never even set foot in the filthy dirty mines, never even gave the workers a thought!

They had "people" to take care of all that nonsense.

It seems like the rich and famous are always talking about "their people".

That makes it sound like their people were slaves. Like the rich owned them. Maybe they did.

Instead of buying humans from slave traders the wealthy just gave the money directly to "their people".

You know the old saying "Cash talks, Bullshit walks"?
All most of us get is a ton of Bullshit, so if you spread around enough cash someone will obey any order.

For whatever reason this line of thought led me to this obvious conclusion.

Thousands of us "little people" risked our lives every day under tons of dirt for a place to live and three squares a day, for us and for our families. Translate "little people" to "middle class".

Remember a lot of what the mines paid us was in script and we repaid the owners when we lived in company shacks, bought company furniture, and ate company groceries? _I can't <u>believe</u> I hadn't seen it before.

We are all slaves!

These rich bastards and the fancy whores they married called giving orders to "their people" An Honest Days Work. I'll <u>tell</u> you what an honest days work looks like to me.

## Chapter 3 Breaking the Chain

I get up at six in the morning to build a fire in the cook stove. My wife, Nora, likes a truly hot oven for her biscuits, and it takes some time for the cast iron stove to get hot.

Unless there has been a good rain overnight I pump enough water to fill the cistern, that large wooden barrel beside the kitchen door.

Next I check the outhouse to make sure there is a good supply of dry toilet paper, and that the john is as clean as it could be.

When those simple chores are done I wash up, eat breakfast and leave the house by seven thirty.

If Nora needs the car (a beat up old Chevy) I walk the two and a half miles out of the holler to meet my fellow miners in town.

We gather in Poormans Pour House, a bar where we all have a drink or two of cheap bourbon while we wait for a truck to pick us up and put us down at the Happytown Mines.

We are mid way from the top of a very high W.Va. mountain when we arrive at the mines entrance, and everyone is loaded into what we call a mantrip. A mantrip is only an old coal car that was too damaged to hold bug dust or even lump coal. The company thought it was just fine to hold humans. I better say "just fine to hold workers."

I'm not really sure the company thought of us as humans.

We took the mantrip straight down a shaft about five thousand feet into the bowels of the mountain.

The car stopped in a huge hollowed out cave, which was the main room.

Many other holes leading to various seams of coal dotted the walls of the main room.

Like rabbits, or rats, each miner knew which hole led to the face he was working.

The face, I'm sure you know by now, is the exposed seam of coal. I had to load coal almost as fine as beach sand.

I worked the coal in my warren by triple sticking the face with T.N.T. to blow the seam to bug dust because the tops of the cars I loaded were just nine inches from the ceiling.

In other spots the ceilings were much higher and those guys were single stick dynamiting the seam then shoveling up the broken coal lumps into an open-top rail car.

We pushed the empty cars up to the face, pushed the filled car back to the main room then pushed another empty replacement to the face. Now that's a hard days work. Sound like something you would enjoy?

I didn't think so.

I really believed what I was told as a kid; that was if I worked hard and was honest I would be successful.

I have never taken a penny that wasn't mine from anyone. I've made sure to return anything I've ever borrowed. Never in my life have I brought false witness against anybody.

I've been a real straight arrow and I've worked hard all of my life.

Now my wife and son are going hungry again tonight.

If this is success I say fuck it.

Today my eyes were opened. Things are different now. For the first time Mortgage Hill has gotten through to me.

The mansions and Bentleys are not to be admired or envied. Those expensive toys need to be understood.

The huge houses are, for the most part, ego boosters. Braggarts bungalows, purposely designed to engender envy in the neighbors and the aggrandizement of the proprietor.

Those Cadillac's and Mercedes Benzes ought to be seen as Pirate ships flying the Skull and Cross Bones.

In the first place, the owners don't do any manual work; much less do they engage in hard labor to earn them. The men with dynamite and digging did the work, and guess what?

## Chapter 4 Awakening

The rich who got the goodies sure as hell didn't treat my co-workers or me honestly or with the slightest bit of respect.

In the mining camps people like me died early from lung diseases caused by the smoke from carbon lamps and coal dust in the air we inhaled while digging for the black gold that bought those costly do-dads the bosses liked so much.

The cost of a garage here, on Mortgage Hill would pay for shoring up the walls and ceilings of all the rooms in the Happytown mine, making everyone who worked there one Hell of a lot safer.

There were companies that tried to make their mines as safe as they could, and still men died in them.

Not all of the owners were like Happytown's. Some of them probably cared if we lived or died.

Yet the people who parked their Jaguars and Bentleys in these Coach houses think they are more successful than I am. Are they actually?

I have a beautiful wife and a healthy son. They both love me for who I am, a loving husband and a proud father.

God knows it's not for my money.

A little loot in my Levis wouldn't be bad I know, but even in our present straits when I come home, with or without good news, my child runs to greet me, and my wife is glad to see me.
I guess success, like beauty, is in the eye of the beholder; on the other hand it could be just what you see from where you sit.

All I know for sure is that I think my family deserves a lot more than I have given them so far.

Yes Mortgage Hill has gotten through to me, to my heart and to my brain.

Finally, after damned near getting killed in the mines, as so many others have, with tons of mountain falling through the ceiling of the room you work in, this fancy part of town has made a real impression on me.

Today my eyes were opened.

In my heart I know this company robbed me of my fair share of the profit for the work I've done.

If I was the only one hurt, if the destruction was only to me, I might be able to live with it.

The truth is they didn't just injure me, and I can't and I won't stand for it!
Their avarice has taken my sons O.S.U. education, and my wife's life long desire for a real house for the family.

Their lust for a black bottom line has even taken my manhood and my honesty.

## Chapter 5 Nothing for Something?

With anger filling my heart and the sun going down the day began to die.

That's when my nefarious plan began to come to life.

Now it is my turn to take back! Night has covered the area now in protective darkness.

Lights were coming on in a number of the dwellings indicating the owners had arrived home.

I searched the street for the houses that remained unlit. There were three of them side by side.

How do I decide which home would be the one to break my legal cherry?

Which of these places tempted me enough to convert me into the criminal life? Each of the three was still dark. I had to choose quickly before the owners came home.

That single word "owners" spurred my action to quit thinking like a law abiding citizen and start thinking like a crook.

I made my decision and moved forward. From coal miner to criminal was an almost instant transformation. At least it was an easy metamorphosis for me.

One more look at the houses and my brain said to pick the one in the middle.

You didn't need to be too smart to figure that out. The other two shielded this house and I could enter from the side door or in the back door without the neighbors seeing me.

I decided to enter from the back of the house and found myself in a mudroom that led directly to the kitchen. Bread and beans be damned.

My first 'heist' found a huge refrigerator and freezer stocked to over flowing with an assortment of food like I'd never seen.

Not even on Christmas or Thanksgiving.

I found a large leaf-bag and took as much from the icebox as I could carry. Since we didn't have a freezer the frozen stuff would thaw and go bad, so I didn't take much of that.

Talk about going bad, have you ever tried Limburger cheese?

Believe me Limburger is an acquired taste.

My first impression of the unusual product was that a skunk must have died in the Fridge. But, if you can get it past your nose your mouth might love it; mine does.

What? I like to try flaky things, even if sometimes they do stink.

Getting back to business, it was just as I imagined. These people had so much money they just left some of it laying around.

I became two hundred dollars richer that night by picking up the "loose change" in bills and coins.

# Chapter 6 School Days

One of the diamond rings I "found" became Nora's birthday gift. She loved that circle of gold and diamonds, but when I put that ring on her finger my wife cried crocodile tears.

My darling Nora knew we couldn't afford such a thing. I hugged her, wiped away her tears, and told her not to worry; things were looking up.

For the first time in a long time we are a happy family.

Home is now a three-bedroom apartment in the county seat. No more tarpaper shacks. No more pissing through the cracks in the wall or freezing your ass off taking a shit in the winter.

We love our indoor plumbing! Our favorites are the automatic washer and drier, and the bathtub and shower. No more going to Goodwill for things we need. Now we can go to Walmart or Target.

No more Happytown furniture or groceries. It's Value City and Kroger's now.

Matt is still going to the same public school, in the same classrooms, with the same teachers.

Now Matt goes to class with cleaner, newer clothes, a barbershop haircut, new shoes, all of the supplies he needs, and one hell of a lot better attitude. Today those same instructors are giving the boy a lot more attention.

Our son is getting a much better education.

Nora has shed a few more tears since I put that first expensive ring on her finger, but now they are tears of joy. Speaking of tears of happiness, my own eyes got misty last night when I arrived home.

I almost cried with pride when Matt swaggered, not just walked, he actually swaggered over to the car and said "Dad, guess what."

"I don't know kid. Did you get an A in Math?" I answered.

"Better than that Pop. I am now a first string member of the Bulldogs basketball team," he said with the biggest smile I had ever seen.

Who says crime doesn't pay?

I've been into the underside of society for sixteen months now and have done forty-eight jobs. Three a month is all we need, and I figured with fewer jobs there was less chance of getting caught.

After doing the break-in that gave Nora her first diamond ring I went "job hunting" in my new endeavor the next day.

When I started looking for honest work I had no qualifications, and got no jobs.

## Chapter 7 Qualifying qualify

When I started my dishonest career I didn't have to know anything about being a crook just how to read; maybe not even that for a snatch and grab thief. Heck, almost everyone is qualified to steal.

I really didn't even know how to pick my targets. I needed a place to plan and think. There was a state park a couple of miles out of town so I decided to make that my headquarters.

My pick of the park was another lucky break for me, because someone had left yesterdays newspaper on one of the green park benches. White on green made the paper easy to spot. I was looking for the sports section when my eye caught a picture of a familiar house in the Society Section.

It was one of the fancy abodes on Mortgage Hill.

The story was a detailed description of the people that lived there and their current plans to go on vacation.

Those society pages told me when and where all of the Hotsytotsys were going on vacation. Valuable information if you are a thief.

I want to thank all of the society page writers for my quick education in burglary.

I should also thank the Radio and TV people for being so thorough in reporting the details of crimes.

Because of slow news days and their need to try to build, or at least to keep, an audience I now know where to buy Marijuana, or how to grow the weed if I wanted it free.

The news anchors taught me how to steal cash machines from convenience stores.
I learned how to use or sell, stolen credit cards if I wanted to, and much, much more, including how to break into homes with burglar alarms.

I am now highly qualified for my new profession. Thank you all.

In my opinion, and now that I have some experience, I am entitled to an opinion, every good operative needs a cover that can be checked if necessary. That lesson was taught to me by one of Matt's teachers.

My son came home from school one day and said his teacher asked him what his father did for a living. Matt told the inquisitive educator that he wasn't sure but that he would find out.

"What do you do Dad?" he asked. "I know you go to work every evening but you never told me what you actually did."

"Well son I'm not particularly proud of being a self employed private investigator," I replied, "I don't talk about snooping into things for my clients.

I work undercover most of the time and the people I work for want me to remain anonymous. If the clients I perform these investigations for knew I told anyone, even you, I could lose my job."

"O.K. Pop, mums the word," Matt said, "I'll tell Teach you work for the government and can't talk about it. But Dad, you should always be proud of a good days work, or in your case a good nights, work," he said with a smile on his face.

Not a bad off-the-cuff answer I came up with was it?

This experience made me give some serious thought to self-preservation.

I remember reading about the government being unable to convict a notorious criminal that was a known murderer, along with many other crimes, until the FBI got the IRS involved.

Between the two agencies they put Segal in jail for life.

I deduced that a guy could escape anything except tax evasion.

Deciding the best tool a thief can own is a checkable legitimate income; and having told my son I was a Private Eye, I became one through a home study course.

Six months and three thousand dollars later my badge and license arrived.

The education did set me back a pretty penny, but it has been many times worth the investment.

I named my new business Phantom Investigations.

# Chapter 8 Things Change

The first official act, and at that time the only one, as a detective was to file income taxes.

I file my taxes every year. On time. Every time. If I do time, it will be for some other stupidity it will not be for tax evasion.

Not long ago I was doing eight hours of hard labor every day, six days a week, earning; and I mean really earning, three hundred dollars per week.

Now most of my labor is only thinking about how to do what I'm going to do next.

My actual physical labor lasts between five and fifteen minutes per job, each job netting between eight hundred and twelve hundred dollars.

All of my life I've heard miners telling other miners to work smarter not harder.

I thought they meant things like using a stick and a half of TNT, or double sticking a face to get smaller, lighter lump to load; or bringing grease in the hole to lubricate the coal car wheels, making them easier to push.

I thought those were the kinds of things that meant you were a smarter worker.

On the other hand now that I give it some consideration, I don't imagine you're being too smart when you're on your knees under five or six hundred tons of coal; with a shovel in your hands, and looking forward to the possibility of dying from black lung. I do see you working hard.

Finally I understand the true meaning of "Work smarter, not harder".

You know that the labor in my new profession is much less intensive. I just carry a large bag, or sometimes a suitcase, to fill with assorted merchandise.

On some rare occasions I don't work even that hard. No, not because my job came up empty. The reverse is true.

Once in awhile I come away with my pockets full of very valuable jewelry. It doesn't take much room to store a three-carat diamond worth forty to one hundred thousand dollars.

Now I am working much easier and banking much more. Does this make me smarter? I think so, but still, I wonder if this is really smarter not harder? That's open for debate.

You may not die of black lung or of a cave-in, however you will die of something.

You will probably enjoy your life better and live longer as a thief than you would as a miner, or for that matter, by working most other hard labor jobs.

## Chapter 9 Tight Spots

On the other hand when you're locked up if you get caught performing illegal acts, you will not enjoy life, possibly not even live as long.

I am not positive of anything, having never been the guest of a state or federal prison, nor have I contracted black lung, or died of cancer, thus far. Nevertheless, I have a very vivid imagination. Prisons are not resorts. I can imagine what might happen to a newby in a jail full of sex-starved men.

I have had some narrow escapes from going to prison.

Once in the very beginning of procuring ill-gotten gains for a living, a lady came home while I was riffling her dresser for appealing jewelry. Of course her home was completely carpeted so she approached in total silence.

Fortunately the reflections in the dresser mirror showed the door to the room begin to move. As the door moved did so did I. Dropping to my knees I got behind an overstuffed chair before she saw me.

When the lady of the house entered her master boudoir toilet, I finished selecting my jewelry in a hurry. When I heard the water flush I left the scene.

If the lady caught me, and managed to keep me in the house 'till arresting officers arrived,

I probably would have been sentenced to live three years, possibly longer, in a state lock-up.

According to all I read or saw on TV or in the movies, three years in a federal prison could literally be a lifetime of dropping to my knees. The thought of that damned near made me quit living a life of crime. Except for the real memories of life on my knees with a shovel in my hand loading coal I might have given the underworld the finger.

That mental image kept me from quitting my illegal activities.

Another close call brought sweat to my forehead just in time. My target was the home of a jeweler, Mr. Hammerschmit, who had taken his family to Europe for the summer.

I surveyed the residence for several weeks before their scheduled departure on a luxury liner. Their house was the largest structure in a ten-block area. The family's transportation was a Rolls Wraith and a couple of MB gull-wing sports cars.

I glanced through a downstairs window while I walked my dog past the Hammerschmit mansion in the evenings.

My observation revealed a TV picture that seemed to cover more area than a cinema screen

Whatever gave me the idea that there might be something inside the place worth stealing?

Was it only a hunch, or maybe it was the cars, or the huge TV?

But the clincher was the three huge Dobermans patrolling the property all night. My mind was set on waltzing past the killer canines to reach my score, and I knew it was impossible as long as those monsters were on the job. So, beddy-by-time was near for them.

I sure as hell hoped those animals liked beefsteak laced with sleeping potion, because they were going to get some.

The ship left the dock with the Family Hammerschmit bound for Kiel at 5:30pm. The sun set at 7:pm.

At 7:15pm the Dobermans ate the bloody meat full of sleeping serum I tossed them. They conked out three minutes later.

At 7:20pm I used a credit card to enter through a side door of the now empty home.

A beautiful set of silverware worth about four thousand dollars found its ways into a black plastic bag I brought with me.

Next I discovered the place where the jeweler's wife hid her extra cash. The money was in one of the few places many women hid money. It was in an otherwise empty sugar bowel on the china shelf. Most men preferred to stash the cash in an old pair of shoes or an empty shoebox in their closet.

According to my Casio, I was in the house for four and a half of my allotted five minutes.

I knew there was almost no time left before the cops responded to the silent burglar alarm I noticed on my way in.

The control box was mounted on the wall of the steps leading to the basement.

It was time for my adieu to the Hammerschmits. I stuffed the cash in a jacket pocket, grabbed the plastic bag with the box of silverware, and was headed for the door when I heard cops coming.

I had under-estimated how quickly the law would respond to a call from the home of a man as rich as Hammerschmit.

.

The Police car, scarcely two blocks away, barreled toward us with sirens screaming, as I was going out the way I came in.

I always wondered why cops make so much noise alerting us criminals that they are on their way?

The black and white was in the merchants driveway several minutes sooner than they would have been in a poorer section of town.

I barely made it behind the bushes ‘till the uniforms were inside the house, searching for the cause of the disturbance.

I was almost certainly going to be caught if I didn’t come up with a plan on the spot.

Wearing reversible Black/White clothing was just one more of the strategies I learned that might keep me out of jail.

Using a reversible black jacket, one side white, should provide great camouflage.

# Chapter 10 Down Time

No thief would wear bright white to pull off a robbery.

I took off my jacket as the sweat broke out on my forehead. Turning the garment inside out I put it back on so the bright white side showed, took a few steps back, and ran through the bushes toward the policeman on guard at the front door of the jewelers home.

"Officer, Officer" I shouted waving the black plastic bag with the silverware in it as I sprinted toward him "I saw someone running from this house dressed all in black, wearing a ski mask."

"When I gave chase they dropped this bag and ran like hell." I said, panting as if trying to catch my breath "just too fast for me, whoever they were. They jumped into a dark Buick parked on the next street over and sped away."

After asking what I was doing in the area this time of day, and being told that I was jogging, they asked for identification, but like most people I don't carry my drivers license or anything else, when I run.

However, using another of my strategies, I gave them my name and address as Karl Julius of 1310 Kingston Rd. (Karl was in the obituary column three years ago)

.

The investigators thanked me for my help, then told me not to leave town. Karl didn't need to leave town since he didn't exist.
Mrs. Hammerschmits sugar bowl gave me ten thousand dollars in one hundred tightly rolled one hundred dollar bills.

Another of the things I learned is to share the wealth! I shared in the Hammerschmit good fortune so I would pass along a portion my windfall to others. The Salvation Army was one of my favorite charities ever since they gave me something to eat and a place to stay after I left home when I was fourteen.

I had no job, I was living on the streets, and I was fighting with my parents.
An officer in that army, who strongly believed in redemption, took me in and urged me to go back home.
Captain Joel Mancusi convinced me to reconcile with my Mom and Dad.
I'm forever grateful to that Captain and to the Salvation Army in which he served. They gave me protection while I regained enough of my self-respect to return to my family. Feeling forever indebted to them, I try to reward their kindness with anonymous donations of One hundred dollars a month. Two hundred in December.

My son, Matthew, furnished his first apartment, Bedroom, Living room and Kitchen, all for a hundred seventy five dollars with some pretty nice stuff from Goodwill.

Now they get a check for fifty bucks a month to help their handicapped workers help others.

Wives of miners injured or killed in mining accidents get some help every month too.

I also donate to Planned Parenthood, ASPCA, and three or four more whenever I can without depriving my family.

My business is doing better most of the time now that my craft is being honed. Actually all I do when my jobs pay well is help the wealthy help the needy.

I know my donors would send the cashiers checks themselves, if they weren't so self-absorbed.
The ones who do contribute to charity for other than tax credits are to be congratulated.

I did leave town with my family for a very well earned vacation at Boca Raton. Nora was on the rag, and I was Horney as hell.

Usually when I get like this I go to work so the feeling would pass.
Not now because we were in Boca, where I had no targets to work.

I thought a long walk might do the trick.
I left the hotel for a stroll beside the ocean, but I didn't make it to the beach. I took a side street and entered a bar.

Instead of the crunch of sand beneath my sandals it was the feel of artificial turf.
Instead of hearing the sound of surf I was listening to a Mariachi band.

As my eyes and ears adjusted to the new environment the softer sound of crying was heard.

Looking for the source of sorrow my eyes fell on a vacation spoiler. The sobs were coming from an attractive, young looking, red haired female.

She sat with an untouched drink on the table in front of her and there were tears running down her cheeks.

I went to her table, pulled out a chair and sat.

The startled young lady turned to me starting to speak. I put my finger across her lips to silence her and said "Shhh. I'm a friend. How can I help you? You look like you could use a friend right now. Why are you crying?"

Her cry got louder, and the tears came faster. She choked out "Who are you, what do you want?" "I told you I'm a friend", I said, "All I want is to help you if there is something I can do."

"No one can help me now" she sobbed, "My little girl is gone and that miserable son of a bitch will never bring her back."

"Slow down a little bit," I urged "Start with your name and tell me who the miserable son of a bitch is and why your little girl is gone."

"You really want to help?" she said as the emotions started to ebb "You actually think there is something you can do?" I showed her my P.I. badge, " I can sure as hell try if I know the whole story." I said, "Now start at the beginning, what's your name?"

"I'm Susan," she answered, "Susan Petorsky. Most people have called me Pet since I can remember. The motherless asshole that took little Maggie is called Dagger but his real name is Don. Donald Skarney. He was my pimp." Susan said. Looking defiantly at me Susan said, "That's right I'm a whore. I've been one since my mother turned me out when I was twelve. Do you still want to help me?" Pet asked, wiping her eyes with a napkin.

"What you do for a living is your business." I told her, "Now tell me more about Dagger."

"What can I say about Dagger except that he's a typical class 'A' pimp?" Susan answered.

"Start from the beginning." I said, "How did you get started selling your body, what's a class A pimp and how, and when, and why, you got started with Dagger.
Also tell me how he is threatening you now." I told her.
"It's a long story," she said.
Going on, Susan was correct. It was a long story, and at times a very sad tale, while at other times it was extremely frightening.

I asked her to wait while I called my wife to tell her I was doing research and would be late getting in.
I told Nora I would see her in the morning for breakfast.

# Chapter 11 Susie Spills All

Returning to Susan I noticed her drink was now half full.

Presumably the missing half was giving her the courage to fill me in on the how, when, and why of her association with Donald Skarney. "From the beginning" she said, starting like stage directors do, "Darla, my dear unwed mother wanted to abort me 'till she found out the government would pay her if she kept me.

This lovely a-moral bitch was herself a street whore who shacked up with a lot of live-in 'boy friends'. On my twelfth birthday her current lover gave me a 'present'. He raped me."

"Darla walked in on him in the act. Instead of being outraged Mom saw his act as an opportunity to put more cash in her pocket. That's right. My first pimp was named Darla, yes indeed, my dear momma Darla started selling me the same night she caught her 'lover' banging me. Momma Darling made me, her twelve-year-old daughter; turn three more tricks that night.

For the next six years I averaged four fucks a night at fifty dollars each. Mommy dearest gave me an allowance of ten dollars a week; and all of the weed I could smoke.

Then came Donald. He came all right, right in my mouth. He must have really liked the head I gave him. His next move was to buy me from Darla.

Skarney paid her five hundred dollars and told her to stay away from me from then on.

Mother proved she loved me a lot. A lot more than five hundred dollars worth anyway. She tried to get a thousand, saying I was damn good at what I did and I would do anything I was told to do.

Donald took a fifty out of Darla's' hand, slapped her in the face so hard he knocked her down, and said she better shut the fuck up or he would take another fifty.

My darling mother had a big guy named Al living with us at the moment and that two hundred pound hulk started moving toward Skarney, ready to beat his ass, right arm cocked ready to drive his balled fist into Donald's gut.

We quickly learned why the street called Donald the Dagger. You guessed it. When Al approached with blood in his eye a long switchblade appeared in Skarneys hand and sliced into Al's right arm. The fat bastard fell down on the floor screaming, blood no longer in his eye but all over the carpet.

Dagger grabbed my hand and dragged me out the door. He took me to his posh apartment on the East side. That night. I learned I would be his slave, his woman, his maid, his whore and anything else he wanted me to be.

The funny thing is that at eighteen years of age, with Donald, I finally learned what it meant to be treated with respect. Dagger did act like he respected me, as long as I did exactly what he ordered me to do.

I was set up in a nice apartment in a good neighborhood.

I was no longer just a piece of street ass. I became class ass.

With Skarney as my pimp I moved off the street to become a prostitute, working customers who came to my apartment, I was getting twenty percent of what they paid for my services.

Next, after being taught by Dagger how to dress, how to apply makeup, and how to perform my duties as if they were gifts to my customers, I became a call girl. Taking dick by appointment only.

I was given thirty percent of the original charge.

Dagger also let me keep fifty percent of any tips.

Woe be unto me however if I disobeyed him.

The first time I nearly disobeyed him my appointment was with a dyke. I hesitated to kiss her cunt. The lez made a 'phone call and in minutes Dagger showed up in her house.

He beat me in front of her and made me lick her pussy. Then I had to French kiss her asshole.

Dagger beat me some more, always hitting me where the bruises didn't show. There were several hours of pain and humiliation.

Not because I <u>refused</u> to do as ordered, but because I <u>hesitated</u>. I know I deserved all that Dagger did to me.

I had no right to even hesitate to follow his customer's desires after all of the good things Donald did for me.

I called him Donald when we were alone in his penthouse.

When I wasn't working he did treated like his girlfriend. Skarney gave me little gifts of candy or flowers when I returned from an appointment.

We attended Broadway shows after a busy week. We dined at fabulous restaurants.

Of course I satisfied his every sexual desire. I began to think of myself as his wife.

I was twenty when he knocked me up. A sonogram showed the fetus to be female.

Donald insisted I keep our baby and while I was carrying he only allowed me to take anal or oral appointments, mostly from women.

Dagger still treated me like a girlfriend for a while after our baby was born. He gave me whatever I wanted 'till I was about twenty-five. I'm thirty now and things are different.

Now I'm just a very talented employee.

Is that the how, when, where, and why that you wanted to know" she asked.

"No, not at all." I answered. "So far it sounds very much like what I would expect a pay-for-pleasure girls life to sound like. You haven't told me how and why Dagger is threatening you now"

"I told you he took my ten-year-old daughter and he won't give her back. The last thing the bastard said to me was he hoped Maggie is as talented as I was."

"That rotten son-of-a-bitch is going to turn her out and she is only ten years old! He's going to make her a slave in a horrible life just like my shitty mother did to me."

"Please, she begged," As the tears began to flow again, "Please, if there is anything you can do to save her from this life, please, please do it. I'll give you everything I have, do anything you want, please I'm begging you."

Tears were now flooding her face and the crying, sniffling, and sobbing started all over again.

When I heard Susan say the word "slave" It solidified my decision. I have never gotten over the feeling I was a slave to J.D. Cooper.

A plan began to form instantly.

First retrieve the kid, and then punish the pimp.

I asked Susan for her address and 'phone number, and I wanted to know where Dagger lived too. I told Susan I would call her soon. It was late now and I was tired. Now for the hotel and a soft bed before breakfast with my family. I left to grab some sleep.

## Chapter 12 The Best Laid

Finding Dagger at work and getting the kid away from him probably won't be a major problem.

I had Skarney's private address, The Carltown House. Considering his profession any cop or cabbie will know him.

The Carltown was one of the oldest hotels in town so there were not a lot of modern security features, which meant there were many ways I can enter if I wanted to.

Not knowing absolutely if little Maggie was being kept in the penthouse or being stored somewhere else waiting to be sold, I decided on a different tack to dull the Dagger

I returned to my hotel to spend some time with Nora and Matt and to explain to them that for me this excursion had turned into a working vacation. After dinner Nora took Matt on a shopping spree while I checked into a different hotel under another name. Afterwards I went to the Carltown to watch for Donald Skarney.

The doorman got a fifty for some info on the pimp and another fifty to keep his mouth shut about me.

Apparently Dagger had never been so generous so I got everything I wanted from the doorman.

He told me when my target left the building, where he went, where he did business, how much he charged the Johns, everything and then some. Edward, the Carltown Doorman, told me that around One O'clock, after having lunch in the hotel, Mr. Skarney left for the Good Angel Bar & Grill where he conducted his affairs.

Eddie also told me that Mr. Skarney charged about a hundred dollars just to talk to him.

I waited in a booth at the Good Angel. When Dagger came in. I asked the waitress to invite Mr. Skarney to join me. She did, he did, and the fun began.

"Are you Mr. Dagger?" I asked. When he acknowledged his name I introduced myself as Karl, Karl Hammerschmit, the name I registered under at my second hotel.

I told the waitress to bring me a double Johnnie Walker Black straight up, also a double Crown Royal, which the doorman said, was the Donald's drink of choice.

Conversation not being the strong suit for either one of us, when our drinks were delivered we got right to the point.

Our little talk started with me saying, "I'm on vacation with the family, and to be candid I am bored to death."

"To bad your family bores you" he said "but what can I do about that?"

"I was asking some girls on the street where I could get some "special" entertainment when your name kept coming up." I said.

"Didn't the ladies you met offer to solve your problem?" he asked. "Well sure," I replied "but to tell the truth none of them looked younger than sixteen." When I'm on vacation I want them fourteen or younger. I get all of the old ass I want back home."

"That's pretty damned young," said the pimp "I don't know any hookers like that, but even if I could find someone who does handle kids that young it would cost you a bundle."

"I didn't expect it to be free." I said, "But what the fuck are vacations for if you don't do something you don't do back home? If you can get your dream, money should be no object."

"Where are you staying?" Dagger wanted to know, "If I run into something I think you'll like I'll give you a call." I gave him the name of my new hotel; my room number, and I gave him a deadline. "Call me quick" I said "My wife wants to go to Argentina at the end of the week. If I don't answer the telephone it means I'm not alone. Leave a message so I can get back to you, meanwhile I'll keep looking."

Some things work better than others. Greed is damn near as powerful as fear.
My parting shot should light a fire under the pimp's ass.

Skarney didn't want to lose this deal. The 'phone rang in my new hotel room within an hour after Dagger had time to check me out a little.

"Karl here" I said picking up the instrument "is my order ready?" "Yes sir" the caller said "and the meat is even more tender than requested, but it is a little bit more expensive.

There are seventy pounds of Prime veal available at fifteen dollars a pound." The voice said, and then continued with "Do you want the package delivered or will you pick it up?" "I'll come by the butcher shop," I said. "I want to inspect the product. If I'm going to pay fifteen dollars a pound I want to make dammed sure it looks good enough for me to eat."

"Excellent" the voice replied, "Very young, very tender, worth every penny you'll pay c.o.d. Once you accept the shipment we'll have a drink to celebrate the transaction," he said. The call was over without even a goodbye.

I left Immediately for the Good Angel. Dagger was standing at the bar. In the event he needed a fast exit, Skarney stood at the end leading to the restrooms and the alley.

The Donald waved me over when I entered the room and I found a double scotch on the bar in front of me beside a color picture of what appeared to be a small, beautiful doll.
A completely naked small beautiful female doll.

"Well, Karl, do you think you will find that to your liking?" Dagger asked. "It certainly looks exactly like what the doctor ordered." I said, "Where is it?" "Not so fast my friend, there's the matter of the c.o.d." replied Skarney.

"You've got to be kidding me" I answered, "I want to see, and feel, the product in private before you get to touch a dime of the grand.

"I can get all of the pictures I want free from the Internet."

Skarney seemed to stiffen up, going into attack mode.
Then he must have thought better of it.
Dagger relaxed as he said, "About the lease, I learned that the unit has never been used in any way. You will be first in the drivers seat, so to speak, you can break it in however the fancy strikes you."

"When and where?" I asked anxiously.
"Whenever," he said, "it's up to you since you're the one in a hurry. One night only, at my ranch about two miles out of town."
"No," I said firmly "I don't like lonely places when I'm carrying cash."

## Chapter 13 Take Home

I continued "I'll send the family ahead to Argentina tomorrow, then you can bring the package to my room around four tomorrow afternoon."

The next statement to come out of Daggers mouth was not unexpected. He said, "Since this has only been around for ten years and is still Virgin merchandise so to speak the investment is larger. Fifteen hundred.

I broke in saying "I know, c.o.d." then "As I said before what are vacations for except to fulfill dreams?

I'll give you two grand if you leave the goods with me for two nights."

"Deal" said the Donald "We will be there at four." The meeting was over. The plan was moving along smoothly. This part of the plan, retrieve the kid, will all be over the day after tomorrow by five.

The next day at exactly four o'clock there was a knock on the door. It was Dagger holding his daughters hand. "This is Maggie" he said "Is she worth the price?" I had seen this little child before. I had seen her naked in a color photograph.

Now she was fully dressed in a cornflower blue pinafore, white calf length stockings and shiny black patent-leather slippers. She looked like she was on her way to church

This was the package for sale.

Mr. Skarney thought his daughter was on her way to be raped and to begin a whore's life filled with pain and degradation, just as her mother's life was.

I knew better. This was the first step. Maggie and her mother would soon be on their way to wherever her mother wanted to go for a new beginning as whatever they wanted to be.

I motioned Dagger and his prisoner into the room,

Expressing my deep satisfaction with his choice of merchandise.

I showed how anxious I was to slate my thirst for illicit sex by thrusting an envelope at Dagger.

"There's a thousand for tonight. You get the rest after she's been here two nights."

"Now get the hell out so I can get started." I said.

Skarney sneered and said "Train her good, get your moneys worth. Teach the brat how to use everything she's got to please a man. I want that kid knowing how to do everything her mother does, and mama does anything you tell her to do."

With that depraved speech he left.

Positive that Dagger would keep watch on my room for a while to make sure we didn't leave; I decided to give him a few hours or so to feel comfortable.

Maggie was told not to be afraid, that no one would do anything to hurt her.
After assuring her that she was safe with me I asked if she was hungry.
When the little girl nodded her head yes we called room service and ordered burgers and fries.
We ate, and watched a little TV.
Maggie took a nap while I called her mother.

I told Susan to pack a bag for traveling, when and where to meet me and, just in case someone was listening in on our conversation, I said that we were going to go to Miami for her daughter.
We met at the Greyhound Bus Station.

Susan and Maggie were overjoyed to be reunited.

I gave Susan a ticket to New Orleans, a prepaid Visa card and said to her "You have chosen not to let your child ever be a slave.
You can also chose whatever kind of life you do want to live. Please make good choices now that they are yours to make."

I watched them board the bus and ride away.

The first part is done. Retrieve the kid.

I wished them good luck as they left.

Now for the second part.

## Chapter 14 Punish the pimp.

When Susan and her daughter left town I went back to my wife's hotel to let her know that all was well.

It was approaching noon the day after the first night, which of course I spent alone. Well, almost alone. Betsy spent the night with me.

When I left for hotel number two I took Betsy with me. Betsy was a small, silenced twenty-two caliber pistol, the size of my hand even with the silencer attached.
She was little but powerful and accurate enough within a ten-foot distance.

I wanted Skarney to go on believing the lie that I was a pedophile.

I ordered breakfast for two to be sent to the room in the morning so if Dagger checked up on how many people were in my room he would think Maggie didn't leave.
I ate, secured the doors and windows and went to sleep.

The next day I did everything necessary to maintain the illusion in the hotel that I continued my possession of Maggie.

I prepared for a visit from Dagger that evening.

It is my firm convictions that scum like the Donald, knowing they cannot be trusted, in turn does not trust anyone else.

My gut told me he would be in my room before sunset to collect payment for the defilement of his child.

I have been thinking like a thief for a long time now. Part of that kind of thought process is to try to accurately predict coming events.

In my mind I tried to see what and how things would unfold when Dagger discovered the truth.

I prepared for the most probable scene as well as getting ready for secondary and possible third events.

I removed my jacket, put on latex gloves, and wiped down any possible fingerprint-bearing surface.

Putting Betsy in my belt at the small of my back, I then draped a towel across the back of a bow-back oak chair. That piece of furniture was between the door and the bright window.

After doing those little but important things I then made certain that I would be in front of windows that were clear of drapery and shades, so the light partially blinded anyone in front of me.

The conditions were now in my favor.

I was ready for a potentially deadly meeting.

Sure enough the sun barely passed meridian when someone tried to enter my room without knocking. Undoubtedly it was Skarney trying to surprise me.

I unlocked the door and stepped back. "Come in" I called. The pimp entered, scanned the space and demanded "O.K. where the hell is she?" His right arm was stiffening, indicating where his switchblade was resting in its spring-loaded holster.

I put both hands behind my back, one hand caressing Betsy. "Where should a ten year old girl be?" I asked, and then said, "She's with her mother."

Dagger unleashed his switchblade and lunged toward me. My practice on the pistol range paid off. Pop, Pop Betsy spit out the hot lead.

One slug ripped through the hand Skarney was holding the deadly steel in. Another 42m piece of hot lead tore a hole in Daggers left knee, dropping the bleeding pimp to the floor.

"Now you slimy piece of shit listen up." I said "if I ever see you again or even hear of you being within a hundred miles of Susan or your little girl, you will think I did you a big favor today."

I continued my dialog, "The next time I'll destroy your other knee, both of your shoulders, and maybe an eye."

"None of my family can stand a son-of-a-bitch that would do what you did to your own daughter so remember you're not safe anywhere."

I said, "That's a fucking promise from the son of the Teflon Don."

I was satisfied with the knowledge that the second part of the plan was done. The pimp was punished. I left for the hotel.

## Chapter 15 Ice & Snow

My family and I left Boca Raton within the hour. As soon as the wheels touched down and I heard the tires squeal on the runway I knew we were home. I also knew we had gone through a hell of a lot of coin in Boca.

It was time to get back to my regular line of work, robbing the rich and helping the helpless. The residents of my current district are not in need, but the malnourished children of Appalachia would most certainly appreciate a good meal. So would my bank account.

More of us need to learn why my savings sock has a hole in it. I learned early on in my present career; it is one of life's greatest lessons that anyone can learn: Do Unto Others As You Would Have Them Do Unto You.

The step after you learn the lesson is to live it. If you do practice what the golden rule preaches you will find, as I did, that the sock never empties.

That hole I mentioned empties directly into my family's expense account bowl, with the excess overflowing into the basin of the bereft.

When that happens a complicated little universal law goes into effect for you.

The edict is, “when you do what you can do you can do more than you do do.”

Hell of a thing to be able to learn any good lesson from criminals, the world’s worst malefactors isn’t it?

Speaking of villains, another peculiar twist to life is that any good criminal heeds the teachings of the political culprits in Washington.

We all know this oft practiced deceit: “Tell the people what they want to hear, then follow the course that puts the most money in your pocket.”

In “third world countries” taking money for political favors by people with special interests is called “bribery”.

In the United States it is called “securing the vote” by lobbyists.

A lobbyist is a person paid by other people with special interests to buy the honor and integrity of politicians

In the underworld it is called “I owe you one” by those of us seeking information or action by other, usually more powerful, members of the criminal class.

So far I have prospered without it being to my advantage to engage in any of these distasteful practices.

I did come close though, when Mother Nature prohibited me from breaking into the homes of the wealthy. She stepped in to make my capture almost inevitable.

Mamma Natural laid down a thick carpet of snow, which would record several clues to any robbery I might perform. The icy crystals could capture Information like points of entry and exit, direction of escape, shoe size and manufacture; Possibly other incriminating information.

Some of the time it is a prerequisite to take a step back in order to move forward. This was one of those times.

I turned the pages of my life all they way in the past to stop at my fifteenth birthday.
That was my age when I found out words are very powerful tools, whether or not the speaker is a liar.

True or false, words will cause people to react to statements that coincide with their beliefs, desires or fears.

Words bring us joy or despair; they are the true instigators of war or the pioneers of peace. These connected syllables convince mothers to send their sons to fight worthless wars, waged for no good reason.

Even if some politicians have declared the legality of murdering another human for whatever flimsy excuse, is there ever a good reason to kill each other?

Little letters tied together seem harmless, but they do make us do the damnedest things don't they?

## Chapter 16 Another Beginning

I needed to change my modus operandi. I can chose anything, salesman, preacher, teacher, accountant or politician. None of which appealed to me, with the possible exception of politician.

Politics has its drawbacks too. I did not want to spend my time, or my money, to take a chance on getting elected to an office from which I could greatly manipulate the populace.

I didn't feel I could refill my personal coffers soon enough on a race it was possible to lose. My remaining choice was to become an entrepreneur in an area that can generate cash quickly.

Theoretically I was already on the right path.

I decided that since I had to change course my best option seemed to be to hang out the P.I. shingle that I earned several years earlier.

Remember my son and one of his teachers guided my steps by asking me what I did for a living? Shortly after their inquiry I graduated from a home study course and became a private investigator. That meant my shingle was established, with several years of history through my tax returns, even if I never was actively employed as a P.I.

Who better to control than someone so insecure they needed to anonymously gain information on something or someone?

The question now became how to launch a fast start?

The answer is, with words, true or not.

The trick is to locate the person's strongest belief, deepest desire or most hurtful fear and to use the knowledge to benefit yourself.

The ability of some of us, politicians as a rule, to play this trick is why otherwise rational people allow their progeny to be murdered in worthless wars, or allow themselves to be exploited.

This was a tactic proven effective to me by what I thought was my good friend, Samuel Johnson.

My friend, Sammy, was always quick to compliment my girlfriend, Anna Lee. He often offered to take us places and show us things.

We were teenagers, Sammy and I, so we were curious about every one and everything including the state of our infatuations. We would have a lot of long talks, sharing our innermost secrets.

One day Sammy approached me with a very troubled look on his face. He was so disturbed when I asked why he was so upset, that my then friend told me he would rather not say.

At my insistence that he tell me what was wrong, Sammy said o.k.

I had to swear never to tell anyone that he told me anything. I swore to keep my mouth shut about he said.

So swearing, I knew that I made Sammy tell me something he didn't want to divulge, a thing he knew would hurt me.

With that my "friend", broke down and blurted out "Anna Lee is cheating on you." Those words crushed me. "No Sammy, you've got to be wrong!" I said with tears welling in my eyes.

"Why would I tell you that if I wasn't positive?" he asked.

That's right I thought why would he say it if it wasn't true?

I had to know what Sam knew that made him so sure.

"How can you be positive?" I asked

Sammy spoke falteringly, choking out words bathed in tears, "Because I saw her making out. Anna Lee was doing it with Johnnie the basketball teams star player."

With those words Sammy hugged me and said, "I'm so sorry".

We both broke down.

Those simple syllables did as they were meant to do. I broke up with Anna Lee, the love of my young life.

Sammy, my erstwhile friend, comforted my ex-girlfriend.

He comforted her right into the back seat of his car time after time until he knocked her up.

That experience with my ex-girlfriend and one time best friend showed me just how powerful words can be.

I know now that there is one word that can change lives forever.

For this word to do its' work it must be spoken in truth

When Sammy left the pregnant girl, and Anna Lee wanted to come back to me she heard this life altering word.

That word is No.

There are other collections of vowels and consonants that do not demand verisimilitude.

They are, in fact, more effective without it.

Suppose for a moment that I was the investigator that solved some well-publicized crimes?

Also suppose I was the P.I. who won a very favorable divorce settlement for a famous couple.

Maybe if I am the one who dug up information about a well-known politician that lost their position due to my investigation?

# Chapter 17 It Works

None of which were true but if you learned of those exploits from a trusted friend would you believe it?

I thought if things like that were insinuated in local newspaper, radio and television outlets it would be enough to attract clients, and to demand large retainers.

Now all I need to do is to determine how I can disseminate the information in an acceptable manner.

Not too difficult if my story is told to them by someone they trust, like their favorite radio or TV news anchor, or if they read it in their daily paper, or see it in a magazine..

The next step will be to create a source those news providers will believe in.

I think if the stories came from the offices of police departments, judges, and senators the news outlets would be happy to use them.

Given that I read newspapers and listen to broadcast news every day, the trusted source became obvious to me.

I would become the “highly placed un-named whistle blower”

.

People believe what they want to believe, need to believe, see on the Internet, or already think.

My 'information' stayed within the bounds of reality and was snatched up by headline hungry reporters that no longer needed additional corroboration, or any real proof, before a story was accepted as actual.

News Directors and Editors didn't need to double-check their favorite reporters either, as long as they could quote a 'trusted source'. If the story was titillating, revealing, horrifying or exclusive it saw the light of day.

One of my planted items simply said, "The very famous couple that you heard about several weeks ago decided on an amicable separation, due to the fact that they were visited by the Phantom."

No actual famous names were mentioned, however a very blurry picture of a couple leaving a notoriously expensive Beverly Hills restaurant accompanied the article. The picture of the couple was so indistinct that they could be anyone you wanted them to be.

The TV Station's report in part was, "Phantom refused to divulge the gory details uncovered in this relationship that we all envied. However we will bring you further details as our WZZXT "A" team uncovers them. In other news…." The extremely sketchy description of the non-event brought the first real customer to the Phantom.

My spurious items in the news paid off better than expected when a stately brunette woman strolled into my newly opened office.
She will remain nameless since she really was the 'companion' of one of the nations respected pre-imminent leaders.

The lady definitely was not a tramp regardless of what the song sang. She did however believe the news, that's how she became - the Phantoms new customer. This lady was very well heeled and utterly powerful.

Her position, as well as her name will go incognito to save us all some embarrassment.

First the well-heeled part. My retainer was two thousand dollars. My fee was one hundred dollars a day plus expenses.

She wrote a check for my retainer as well as two weeks fee also two weeks expenses.
Since we didn't know what the expenses were to be, the lady said I was to consider the check simply a down payment.

The amount written on that light green piece of paper was so large that I considered half of the check a gift to the Appalachia Service Project, the Salvation Army, Goodwill, Coal Miners Relief and some other charities. As far as power is concerned, in addition to the check I was told if there was <u>anything</u> I needed that was inaccessible to let her know, and she would make <u>whatever</u> it was available to me. Is that power or what?

My initial assignment was to determine without question if her “significant other” was also enmeshed with a world famous actress. That was information I could obtain on film in about two days.

Because the Phantom is a really meticulous investigator it took three weeks and another two thousand dollars in expenses to take a picture of the beautiful actress and the lady’s man.

The gentleman was kneeling between the motion picture stars spread legs with her pubic hair in his mouth. Would you call that being enmeshed?

My client did.

Our first client must have been more than satisfied with the Phantoms results. There were many more high dollar cases coming in from her word of mouth recommendations.

The Board of Directors of a chain of banks gave me one of my more interesting assignments. They wanted to know if their Chief Executive Officer, Lorna Cunningham, was embezzling.

Again it was a problem with a fairly easy solution. I took a month to resolve the question. She was.

# Chapter 18 Deposits?

The first anomaly to ring my bell was the fact that deposits in the C.E.O.s checking account rarely fluctuated. The balance was always large enough, or larger, to match her paychecks. There were conspicuously few withdrawals.

Miss Cindy Cunningham never spent very much. According to her paper trail. Not nearly enough to cover her lifestyle.

Don't you think the banks auditors might question that? The board knew the C.E.O. paid cash for her Cadillac and Jaguar. It was considered a normal way for one in her position to purchase transportation. .

If the board had asked the right questions it would have learned that the lady had a significant other. Lorna's live-in lover Mona Cindy also needed an automobile.

The dyke also preferred chariots that were not encumbered. An additional large expense was the four thousand dollar monthly apartment rent the C.E.O. paid yearly. With cash.

The currency for these fun things to keep her lover happy was amassed by the ten percent interest the banks paid the C.E.O. on the many small, imaginary, savings deposits of nine thousand dollars each. These non-existent riches were spread throughout all of the bank branches. Being below ten thousand dollars each meant they were never scrutinized.

The on-paper-only deposits totaled two million dollars. I could hardly believe the financial institution accepted these figures as common for their top echelon people.

Banks allowed ten percent interest to be paid to their V.I.P.s. That generated more of my anger.

I knew the rate on savings accounts for the rest of us was a magnificent one and a half or two percent.

I sold my services short this time, but I sure as hell will remember these figures the next time a bank needs my help to investigate anything.

The next time came sooner than expected. You probably heard or read about this case. I think it probably would have been better off left to a public police department.

In spite of the extensive news coverage you may still not know the truth.

You shouldn't feel bad though; we are rarely told the truth in the news these days because the people making the news are often liars.

You heard that a Fifth National Bank manager, Charles Harsh, was forced to open the institutions vault to a bandit or face the murder of his wife and two small children.

The criminal's accomplices held the family at gunpoint in the manager's house while Mr. Harsh took the lead bandit to the bank and committed the crime.

The police report disclosed that the bank manager had not only refused to cooperate with the crooks, he attacked the leader of the thieves. Harsh stopped fighting with the man when he heard the gunshot that killed his wife.

Fearing for the lives of his two small children Charles then helped the murdering mobsters carry out the robbery that had the nation shedding tears of sympathy for the heroic bank manager.

Mister Harsh was so distraught he was of little to no help to the police investigation. Charles remembered only that the thieves all wore latex gloves and one of the trio was black.

The crime went unsolved. The banks largest depositor, Demitri Romonopoulos, went unsatisfied.

Enter the Phantom.

Mr. Romonopoulos preferred to be addressed as Dimitri. He was a strange sort of billionaire.

Dimitri was known as the nations largest car dealer, with forty five hundred dealerships selling every brand of automobile manufactured in any country. Romonopoulos drove a Chevy Impala onto our parking lot.

He came to my office in search of retribution, not reimbursement. Dimitri wanted to know who did it and why the outlaws were not incarcerated. Cost he said was of no consequence in this investigation, only results counted.

# 19 Big Little Girl

The King of Cars put his money where his mouth is. Fifty-K up front fifty more on delivery of the information. There were very few conditions. No arrest or conviction was necessary.
Only rock solid facts. Face to face confessions paid a bonus.

WTF, I thought, I might confess myself for that kind of cash.-

A good Private Eye, a consciences Politician, and a good News Director are triplets in their methods. The basics of any inquiry or report includes the three Ws, What happened, Where did it happen, When was it done.

All of the great investigators added three more. They are Who did the deed, Why did they do it, and What can be done about it? We try to make Phantom one of the great ones, and we like to think we are succeeding.

In this case here's what we know about what happened:

(1) A murder was done. {Mrs. Harsh was shot to death}

(2) A bank was robbed. {Fifth Nat'l vault, safety deposit boxes etc.}

(3) An extortion was performed {Help us or lose your family}

(4). An abduction occurred {the children were taken}

(5) An escape was successful {the crooks got away with the loot}

(6) Mr. Harsh was of little help {they wore gloves, one was black}

(7). A police investigation was fruitless {No arrests, no clues}

(8) A powerful man was pissed-off {Dimitri Romonopoulos}

We know where that's leading.

(9) The Harsh home {1545 Homestead Park, Sinsonatti Ohio} was the base of operation for the thieves.

(10) The bank {5 Washington Square, Sinsonatti Ohio} was targeted.

(11) Where planning for the operation took place {address unknown} or whose scheme this was.

We know when it happened:

(12) The home was entered 10:30am 07/31/16 {according to Mr. Harsh}

(13) They left by 12:48pm 07/31/16. {According to Mr. Harsh}

The police report had most of this information; we would fill in the blanks.

Now all we needed was the Who and why:

(14) At the scene: Charles and Charlene Harsh, Julie and Jimmy the Harsh children, the killer that murdered the wife, the killers accomplice who watched the kids, the extortionist that went to that bank with Charles}

Again according to Mr. Harsh the killer, accomplice, and extortionist (one thought to be black) are all nameless as of yet.

(15) The reason/reasons for the atrocity {Avarice? Jealousy? Revenge? Hate? Envy?}

There is no motive at this time other than Greed, which doesn't seem like enough reason for this incidence. Upon inspection of the fifteen points of the crime available to me at the moment no loud bell rings.

There is however an uneasy feeling that something is amiss. WHO may not be that difficult, but WHY at this minute seems to be the ball-buster. The murder felt inappropriate. The time struck me as incongruous.

This whole damned thing rankled my ass and stunk of bizarre circumstances. That was the stink of deep dark mystery.

Phantom was more than willing to hold its nose and wade through the obnoxious stench of mystery in order to inhale the sweet aroma of satisfaction. That was the aroma of the Dimitri Romonopoulos gratitude.

There was small chance at this stage to determine the WHO with no D.N.A., no fingerprints, literally no nothing in the Police reports.

I decided to attack the problem like I did my very first crime. I started with the WHY.

Whenever a spouse is murdered the other half of the couple is the first to be suspected, with good reason.

The partner is the person who committed more than seventy-five percent of the homicides as stated in F.B.I. statistics. Also most of us don't know <u>how</u> to commit a murder or how to get away with the act.

Normally spousal deeds are acts of passion and require no knowledge of how to kill or how to escape. Then again, most of us don't know how to <u>solve</u> a murder either.

Thank God Phantom is a fast study. For the kind of cash Dimitri is anteing up I'm going to learn how to catch a killer. Incidentally, I'll likely learn how to <u>be</u> a killer in the process.

Steps to earn One Hundred Thousand Bucks PLUS possible bonuses!

(1) Check suspect's contacts {primary source is telephone calls}

(2) Check co-workers. {All bank employees}

(3) Check personal contacts {store clerks, branch workers, doctor, etc.}

The fastest, best way to establish contacts is through answering the question from whom did they take calls, and who did they call?

A list of called and received 'phone numbers, both cell and land line, were obtainable on the Internet. That is where I would start.

My first search, 07/01/16-07/31/16, was productive:

821-2300 was called 15 times.

116-3612 was called 06 times

261-8780 was called 08 times

Various other numbers were called less than three times in that same period. Interestingly enough the 821-number was listed to a Marcus McPea, the Dolltown Commissioner of Police.

Of extreme curiosity to me, is that several calls were made shortly after Mrs. Harsh was gunned down. Calls to the 821 number were always placed between eight am and six pm.

Those are working hours for a bank manager and for the listed recipient.

Also getting my attention was the fact that none of the 'phone numbers were listed to a Police station or to a Department of Justice.

Conclusion number one is that these contacts were not with The Commissioner but with someone in the Commissioners home. Questions raised? Who and why? This material places steps two and three on the back burner. Step one demands a more exhausting search of the Dolltown address.

I could gain some knowledge by looking up last year's census but I desired more current information.

I particularly wanted the facts about the residents of the commissioner's home during the days those telephone calls were made and received.

My suspicions were aroused from a few of the communications lasting nearly two hours. Who would occupy McPea's instrument like that when he was not home, and what subject would be so absorbing?

My first guess is that a teenager lived in the house and engaged in 'phone sex.

Ahhh, intuition, ain't it great? If only guesses were evidence our courts wouldn't be so jammed up. We found in addition to Mr. and Mrs. McPea there were three other full time occupants of the residence. They were children, all under twenty years old, two sons and a daughter. Charles and Angelina never produced offspring together but each of them did become natural parents with other partners.

Denise was the daughter of Charles with his ex-wife Rita Rose. Angelina was called Angel; a true misnomer if ever one existed. James and Jon were the slightly retarded twin sons of Angel with an unknown man.

In the two-week vigilance of the home the prevalent Mrs. McPea left each morning and didn't return until about four in the afternoon.
This fact ruled her out of the suspect line-up. She was gone during the time of the curious 'phone calls. Phantom discovered where and with whom Angel spent her time away while Mr. McPea dispensed justice.
Hopefully it will not be necessary to divulge the revelation during this investigation.

The possible conversationalists are narrowed to three, two of whom are nearly retarded. That leaves one, Denise. Dee is seventeen, blonde, built, and bursting with sexual energy. BINGO.

Charley Harsh was not likely to spend two minutes, much less two hours, on the telephone with a retarded male. Certainly not four days after his wife was murdered.

This deduction takes James and Jon off the hook too; leaving Denise to be the last piece of bait dangling in the muddy waters.

Giving credence to the facts discovered so far, as hot as Denise appeared to be, it was not beyond the realm of the possible that a man of roughly forty years of age was having an affair with a nineteen-year-old blond.

Now to prove the hypothesis.

Proof is most easily obtained by observation so I started to look first at Denise. Charlie Harsh was not the only person sweet Denise shared time with on Edison's invention.

She spoke to several different male as well as a few female voices.

My snooper 'phone was recording as well as on speaker which enabled me to ignore calls to the McPea home until the correct voice was heard.

Electronic monitoring of all incoming and outgoing messages was quite revealing.

## Chapter 20 Mystery Mr.

One guy's voice was memorable.

This man's voice carried a special sound, containing a vocally mature quality.

I placed the man in his forties, perhaps even fifties.

The blonde's apparent penchant for older men pushed me closer to believing the theory evolving that D.D. could be having a hot and heavy connection to Harsh.

My guess that those long calls to and from Denise's number were about 'phone sex was spot on.

This hard-edged voice was precise in describing sexual acts that he required Denise to perform for him.

He never asked "will you" and not once did he say "I would like you to" do or say or dress as he described.

It was always "you will" do this or that or the other in order to keep him interested enough to continue their relationship.

Other questions now popped up like whack-a-moles.

Who was this caller?

Why did he issue commands for the sexual favors he desired?

Why didn't the girl object?

Where did Denise venture off to when she went out after that persons pornographic 'phone call?
Was the man actually, as I presumed him to be, in his mid forties or early fifties?

Later in the day the mature voice was heard again.

Denise answered the ring, "Hello Mr. I stayed here waiting for your call like you told me to."
The male voice, that I too was waiting to hear, said, "Of course you did. You will go to the tennis court in the 18th street Park." He instructed her. Continuing he ordered "Be there at seven thirty, be ready." He concluded.

With what sounded like a happy note in her voice Denise said, " Yes Mr. I'll be ready." The call ended. It was six forty five. I left for the park driving my black Ford Coup.

The name "The Eighteenth Street Park" brings a certain lilt with it don't you think? Situated just eighteen streets from the center of town, yet evoking visions of lakes, wide open spaces, walking and bike trails, baseball diamonds, football fields, tennis courts, and large expanses of grass. All surrounded by the tall buildings of the city. Nothing could be further from the truth.

The Eighteenth Street Park was an open area in a forest. At one time in the distant past, It used to be the St. John farm; a few acres of plowed farmland in the middle of an extremely large stand of Oak trees.

Farmer John St. John gave the property, with caveats, to the local church.

One stipulation was that the property be used to provide a recreational area, a park, for all citizens not just the parishioners.

Another condition was that a specified acreage remains uncut.

If the trees were felled the church would suffer a penalty of one hundred thousand dollars plus interest to be paid to the St. John heirs.

The Elders gleefully accepted the land without hesitation, and installed a small lake for bathing and fishing.

Swimming au-natural was no problem for the church as long as men and women came at different times, which did not always happen. The boys and girls soon learned the curtain of woods surrounding the shore made the water perfectly private.

The kids loved to swim; or did they swim to love? Does it matter?

In later years the water was drained and land sports prevailed. Later still the Tennis courts made their appearance, tucked away amid the Oaks. Today the park is an even more perfect place for a tryst, since it is not well maintained few people ever go there.

When John St.John offered the gift to the city the Elders thought the one hundred thousand dollars plus interest stipulation was a joke.

No one laughed when a developer wanted to bulldoze the lovely property so he could transform the site into the 18th St. Mall. This name is less than lyrical.

"18th Street Mall evokes a far different mental picture than it does when you hear "18th Street Park". When you think of a Mall you see Buick's replacing the birds, and the odorous effluent of exhaust pipes replaced the delicate aroma of flowers, while the raucous shouts of shysters replaced calls of the wild raccoons, and other woodland animals.

John St. John did turn over in his grave to reach out and stop the desecration. The reason for the cities sobriety concerning the sale of the city park was simple. The St. John heirs demanded two trillion dollars, in advance, before a single tree could be removed. Interest is a bitch, huh?

This evening Mr. St. Johns, last gift to the people, his woods, provided excellent cover for Black Beauty. My rearing stallion is my little black coup. Yes, the name given to my small car came from my lack of imagination. I copied the name from the marvelous book "Black Stallion" by Anna Sewell, which I read as a kid.

The oak grove is a wonderful blind from which to spot prey. I parked Black Beauty at seven fifteen. My elfin machine vanished in the shadows under the Oak trees as I had noticed wrens do just after they entered a bush.

The extra quarter hour I gave myself before 7:30 I used to determine the owner of a blue Cadillac Seville parked near the tennis courts.

Searching the B.M.V. with the license plate numbers of the Caddy it turned out to belong to P.J. Phillips, Doctor of Psychology for the Department of Corrections.
A rapid search on Google dug up his short resume.
A matter of great interest was that the man of mind-over-matter science resigned from his last position in Cutland.
No reason given.

A 'phone call to the Cutland Department of Human Services will answer that question tomorrow. How time flies when you're having fun finding facts. Denise turned up just as the Friend of Freud stopped bouncing tennis balls off of the backboard.

It was time to turn on the parabolic microphone and eavesdrop on what I want to be a truly informative conversation. I split the mikes input jack and shared the conversation I would hear on my headset with a recorder. I wanted to preserve whatever transpired in case I needed proof later of the statements they made.

A conversation is two or more people engaged in the polite exchange of factual information, ideas or beliefs. What I heard and recorded from that perverted pair was not polite.

This was more like an interrogation and a dispensation of assignments by a manic teacher; followed by an unquestioning agreement, and instant consummation, by a student ardently willing to satisfy the Instructor.

Phillips walked to his car without a hello or even a glance Denise's way as she approached him. Leaning against the front fender of the sedan the psychologist started speaking, "According to the television and radio news you and your puppets followed my instructions well. You did good. Relax."

Darling Dee smiled from ear-to-ear as the saying goes and sat on a bench designated for tennis fans.

"Thank you Mr." She said.

P.J. spoke, "Did Harsh give you the jewels to bring as I instructed?" "Yes sir," she replied.

P.J. asked, "He mailed the bearer bonds when you left the bank?" "Yes sir." she replied.

P.J. "The cash is still safe where I told him to hide it?" "Yes sir." she replied.

Steps two and three of my search schedule are no longer useful. We had all we needed. Absolute proof of Charles's reciprocity and P.J.s role as ringleader now established it was time to pack up and leave.

Just as I was about to call it quits for this surveillance, I heard P.J. voice over the parabolic mike.

"It is downright incredible what an older man will do when he thinks a young woman loves him." He said.

Denise "Yes sir. I told him how much I loved him when we opened the safety deposit boxes and, I fucked him in the bank like you told me to do. You were right again Mr. That did make the old bastard work faster."

P.J. impatiently, "Yes, yes, you did well. Now you probably want a treat just because you did as you were told."

"Oh thank you Mr., thank you." She said happily.

"Denise." The psychologist said thoughtfully", he continued "Your name sounds much like "the knees" doesn't it?"

"Yes Mr., it does," came the hurried reply, as the girl slid off the bench to her knees.

"Come over here. Now!" came the stern words from Phillips. Dee started to rise and go to the automobile as ordered when P.J. interrupted her. "Did I tell you to stand up?"

"No Mr. I'm sorry. Please forgive me Mr." Came the reply as Denise went back to her knees and began to crawl over the six or seven feet of gravel to her master for the hoped for goody.

She stopped at his feet and looked up to him, expectantly. Much like your favorite puppy might look at you.

"You may unzip my shorts and release my dick." This bogus healer said it like he was bestowing a rare honor upon her.

Denise breathlessly complied, holding his penis in both hands as if it was something precious. She raised her eager, questioning eyes to meet his. "Beg for the rest of your reward" was the answer.

Tears were spilling from her eyes as she implored the renegade psychologist. “Please, please allow me to suck your cock until you fill my mouth with your cum. Please Mr., cum in my mouth.”

“I will this time,” Was his condescending answer, “ but be more obedient in the future.” “When I’m finished with you, put the jewels in my car on your way out.” he ordered as her head began to bob up and down in the act of fellatio.

I returned to my office and tried to make a coherent report out of the salacious happenings of the night. Things began to clear up.

With the revelation of this Sadist/masochist relationship. Another question presented itself. Do her helpers share these peculiar traits too, I wondered?

My next move was to make sure my hunch about the marionettes was correct. After tying strings to Harsh, logic told me the Puppeteer likely dangled Angel and the nearly retarded twins from the control bar also.
Having already cleared Mrs. McPea, only the twins remained to be positively incriminated. The boys were seldom left alone, but when Angelina was gone and P.J. summand Denise, then James and Jon would be by themselves, at least until four o’clock.

It won’t be long until I’m able to obtain an interview with the kids. Past performance told me Phillips demanded that Denise give him sexual satisfaction two or three time a week.

The opportunity presented itself a few days after my recording session. P.J. summoned DeeDee to perform for him around one o'clock.

I gained entrance to the home by telling the twins I was getting information for a movie about them and their sister. They were overjoyed. The boys actually loved their stepsister. John told me all of the good things she did for them.

Denise took them places; she bought them video games, and Dee Dee taught them things. She was fun. Where did your sister take you?" I asked. James told me "Mostly to the movies." Jon chipped in "War movies and gangster movies a lot." "What kind of video games did you play?" was my next question. "Ones like in the movies" was the answer from James. "Yeah, shoot-em-ups is what she called 'em" Jon said, giggling.

What Jon replied caused my ears to perk up. Jon said, "Only we could be part of the movies. We could do the shoot-em-uppin' and when they got up we'd shoot 'em down again."

"Shut up kid." His brother said, "Everybody knows that." "Tell me James" I said, " What does everybody know?" "You know," he said, "How they just play at dying and later get up and get back in the game. Deesy taught us that."

"We even tried it" Jon said enthusiastically "I shot James and he got up, didn't you James?"

"Yeah, but we were in the game." He answered. It occurred to me that these kids never heard of blanks.

My puzzle was complete. Phantom had the solution to the murder/bank robbery. All I needed now was to verify my facts. Time to visit Charles Harsh in person.

.

Entering the Fifth National Bank I inquired from the first teller I encountered about the location of Mr. Harshe's' office.

She told me Charley occupied the third floor corner suites overlooking the city. That's right, suites, plural.

The entire end of the building facing the street, corner-to-corner was the private domain of the son of a bitch that had murdered his wife, robbed the bank, screwed Denise, and thoroughly angered Romonopoulos.

So far Charles had gotten away with it.

Now it's his turn to get angry, get screwed, get robbed of his loot and possibly get murdered, if Dimitri has his way.

The elevator deposited me on the third floor and I walked past Harshe's secretary into the huge office without being announced.

Startled, Charles looked up from his desk asking, "Can I help you?"

"Yes" I said, "you sure as hell can, and I might help you keep on living."

"What do you mean? What are you talking about? Who the hell are you? What do you want?"

## Chapter 21 Movies Anyone

"You ask too many fucking questions. Sit down and shut up, I have something to show you." I replied as I opened my laptop computer carrying case. "You better close and lock your office door"

"Who do you think you are to tell me what to do?" Harsh wanted to know "I'm the President of this bank. You can't order me around.

Get your ass out of here before I call the police." He demanded

"It doesn't make a damn who I am," I said, then "Call the cops if you dare, but tell me something first. "Can Denise McPea order you around about everything or does she just tell you when to put your cock away?"

All of the color left his face when Harsh fell into his overstuffed office chair. "Wh, Who is she?" he stammered.

"How could you forget Delightful Denise?" I asked. Continuing to unpack my computer case. I said "Dee Dee is the little piece of ass you fucked in the vault when you two were opening the safety deposit boxes.

If you don't want her to order you around, how about her Master? The dishonorable Psychologist, P.J. Phillips?"

"I..I..I don't know what you're talking about" he stammered out in a weakening voice.

"You will in a minute asshole, I've got it all on video" I said.

As we were watching the incriminating video I had to explain a few things to the murderous banker; I told him what P.J. meant by Dees 'puppets',
the answer is Phillips meant him and her other conspirators.
I explained why the putrid psychologist was giving orders to the love of the banker's life.

Harsh nearly passed out when he learned the doctor is a sadist, often known in sexual circles as a 'master', and why she accepted his orders without hesitation?

When I told him Denise is a masochist, a person who loves to be hurt and humiliated, also called a "sub",

Bank President Charles Harsh began to cry. Super Sleuth Phantom began to count his fee.

Next a face-to-face confession is in order, to reveal what Dimitri thinks is an appropriate bonus.

Mr. Romonopoulos took the call from Phantom with "Tell me what I want to know."

"How about telling you that Charles Harsh, the Fifth National C.E.O. is with me now to give you some important information?" I said into the intercom.

Dimitri answered. "You know I don't want updates, I want results."

I said, "I'm not here to waste our time, I am here for a bonus."

A buzzer sounded instantly and the door to the inner sanctum opened. I entered Dimitri's office, practically dragging Harsh behind me, and said, "O.K. tell Mr. Romonopoulos your side of the story, or do you want me to run the video show first?"

"Where should I start?" he whimpered.

"Take it easy Charley," Dimitri said. He continued, "No one in this room is going to hurt you. We are all familiar with the facts of the event. Why don't you tell us the details?"

"Start with when and how you met the Police Commissioners daughter." I said.

Harsh began. "It really was love at first sight", He continued telling his side of the events. "At least Denise told me that's how it was for her.
On my part I considered it nothing short of a miracle that she fell for me.

"Denise approached me in the bank, asking about opening an account.
We left the lobby to go to the more confidential confines of my office. That's where this mess all started.

I sat down, ready to help this beautiful young lady fill out the necessary forms.
She leaned across my desk, letting the front of her blouse dip from her shoulders.

I had an unobstructed view of her bare breasts. After taking note that even her nipples were exposed I forced my gaze to focus on her face.
I saw her golden eyes lock onto mine.
They were the most beautifully unusual eyes I had

ever seen. The combination of those penetrating eyes and her stiffly erect nipples gave me a rock hard dick pushing the zipper of my trousers, begging for release.

Stretching even further across the oaken expanse, Denise looked for and found the results of her machinations.

It was the large tent caused by the pole of the hard-on in my pants. She came all the way across the desk then saying, "Wonderful Charles, you do like me as much as I like you."

Those words stunned me. Particularly since I had no idea who she was. " What do you mean, "as much as you like me?" "I've never seen you before in my life." I said.

"Yes you have, in Daddy's office. You came to see Daddy about a phony check passed through your bank. I was introduced to you as his "little girl" that would turn sixteen in two days."

"You may not remember me" she said, "but I sure do remember you." I must have beamed as my chest swelled when the sexy under-age nymph kept flirting with this middle-aged dullard.

"You are the handsomest man I have ever laid eyes on," she purred, "Now I want you to be the handsomest man that has ever laid me," She said, "Lock the door, we don't want to be disturbed for the next hour or so." Denise began disrobing.

The young blonde girl removed her blouse and displayed those tantalizing, bare tits to me.

Forty two years of my life passed by with nothing this exciting going on in even one of the twenty two million, fourteen thousand, seven hundred forty of the minutes in those years. Nothing! Until my key turned in her lock.

Looking at the now naked body of this seventeen-year-old seductress drained all of the reason from my brain. It is unbelievable, but she unbuttoned my shirt, she rubbed her nipples hard against my naked chest, she unzipped my trousers. When this dazzling young lady slipped her hand under my shorts, I believed."

If something like this happened to you, I'll bet you'd do what I did too." Charley said to us.

I can hardly understand what I heard Dimitri say as he put a hand on Harshe's shoulder. He said "Charles, I can see why you would be tempted into intercourse with the girl, but why robbery and murder?"

I was astounded! Dimitri spoke to this scum with compassion in his voice.

"Mr. Romonopoulos, Denise came to my office almost every day." the pedophile said, "After we had sex Dee started telling me how much she loved me.

Every time, while I recovered from our activity, Dee Dee talked about what a wonderful life we would share if only I was rich and single.

"There is a way to make it happen you know," she said. "You run a bank and there are a lot of divorce lawyers looking for work."

Denise would laugh and kiss me. "Think about it. Think about how much better your life will be when you are married to me. Hmm?"

Night after night in bed with Charlene, all I thought about was getting divorced, getting rich, and getting Denise. Soon I entered into the fantasy with my lover; with the fortune we'd get from the bank I would divorce my wife and marry Denise.

I was convinced we would be safe no matter what we did; After all, her daddy was the Police Commissioner, and he'd cover for us wouldn't he?

That was the master plan. Denise got her brothers to help us. She did the thinking, made all of the plans. Dee Dee even procured the necessary tools. Every step of the way Dee assured me of our success. No one will be hurt she promised. It's just an in and out job. Simply in and out. "You know like you in and out me whenever you want to." she said and giggled.

Harsh asked, "Do you think either one of you are strong enough to turn away from that sort of coercion?

I don't think you are. You don't know what the physical love of an astoundingly sexual teen age girl will do to a man nearing middle age.

Sex with Denise is true time traveling. Years melt away, you feel like you did when you were twenty-five. You are Strong, vibrant, capable again.

Neither one of you has ever lived the experience. You've just heard about it." the broken man continued, "What I listened to that you did not hear, are the seductive words of love she whispered in my ear, the sexual practices she

suggested.
I fulfilled desires for Denise that I never did, or would do, with anyone else in my life.

Things I thought of as "dirty" before now became expressions of my love. The amorous sound of her moans when I gave her cunnilingus, made a thrill run through my entire being.
When Dee Dee screamed with pleasure as I brought her to climax after climax, it was validation of my love and of my power.
The smooth, soft feel of her skin, the intoxicating smell of her hair, the soul satisfying taste of Dee Dee's body made me lose all semblance of intelligence.

I become an animal obeying her every command."

Romonopoulos asked in a gentle voice, "Did her orders include the requirement that you murder your wife?"

Harsh replied whimpering, "I swear to God I didn't know they were going to shoot her. Denise always said I would divorce Charlene not kill her."

I stopped him before he went on by saying "You sure as the devil don't act like you are terribly broken up over her death."

"I'm telling you guys the absolute truth here," he said. "I won't stop now. I'll tell you the truth about this as well."

Now the C.E.O. reverted to a steadier voice "I'm not at all disturbed. Charlene meant nothing to me for years before all of this shit happened. When Dee Dee walked into my life I admit the door was wide open. I gave no thought at all to Char. I fell so deeply in love with Denise that when the gun went off I was surprised, but then again I felt no sense of loss, my feeling was one of relief."

I wanted to kick the son of a bitch in the chops for talking about the mother of his children like that, and I was about to do just that, when the Greek spoke up. "So Miss McPea owns the murder in addition to the robbery and all the rest of it?" Dimitri reflected. "You are the innocent one dragged along by lust?"

"No, not all of it." Was Charley's prompt response, "I am guilty of bad judgment, along with gullibility for believing a girl like Denise actually could really love me that much."

"You ignorant motherless bastard." I was falling off a verbal cliff, and I couldn't stop myself, "That little cunt never loved you at all."

"Shit, she didn't even like you. Denise is a Sub, a masochist, a slave following the commands of her Master."

Again I didn't hold my tongue, "Don't forget your unadulterated fucking stupidity too.

Not only was I hoppin' mad, I was spewing out profanity as a second language.

I can't fathom a well respected, legitimate bank such as Fifth National being run by such a dumb son of a fatherless-prick like you are."

Still descending the cliff of verbal abuse, I said, "The teenage whore would fuck a box full of snakes and suck off the entire Cutland Musketeers basketball team during half time if "Mr." even mentioned that it might amuse him to see her do it."

"Mr." was the name her sadist Psychiatric owner allowed her to use when addressing him.

"Are you finished chastising Mr. Harsh?"
Bam! I hit the bottom of my understanding.
That criticism of me came from Dimitri!

The single answer I could think of was "Bullshit."

Romonopoulos continued speaking, "Mr. Harsh, thank you for coming clean about this whole sordid affair.
I promised you that no one in this room would hurt you if you confessed, so you are free to go" said the King of Cars.

Free To Go! The words made my ears want to ignite and burn off my head. Free to go? After all Harsh had done?
My noggin began spinning on my shoulders when Mr. Billionaire told Charles he would be escorted out of the building and driven to where he needed to be.

Is this what Dimitri was paying more than half a million dollars for? An admission of guilt and a half-hearted apology from a spineless pedophile?

It doesn't look to me like Harsh will get his just rewards.

Well, what the hell, I thought, I'll get my payday; I hope Romonopoulos got his moneys worth.

The chauffer who entered the room for the first time to take 'Mr. Harsh' to the limo looked like a WWF star.
"This way sir," the driver said as he opened the door for Harsh.

When the office door was shutting I heard Dimitri say under his breath, "first stop hell."

My head stopped spinning, my ears cooled off and I felt fifty thousand times better. "Where is hell Dimitri?"

The Chevy driver laughed as he said, "Someone who was not in the room with us took Harsh to a very secluded small ranch I know of."

With that the King of Cars wrote Phantom a last check adding twenty-five thou to my fee for the face-to-face bonus.

Sanity, once more, rules my life. I'm home again. The weather is all blue skies and white clouds during the daytime now. When the sun goes down those same skies are a clear black background for millions of sparkling stars.
We have Lover's nights with picnic days.

## Chapter 22 One Window Closes

Things are right with the world again. My kid has a terrific future, my wife is more loving than she has been in years, and my health is excellent. I am not in danger of being incarcerated at the moment.

Phantom has more potential clients than we can possibly accept, and money is no longer a problem.

Everything seems to be going great. Isn't this a time for celebration? Still, something is not right. It feels like there is a monster deep in my psyche gnawing at my intellect, releasing my feelings of discontent.

On the other hand, this devil could be a messenger-angel knocking on my sub-conscious, asking what problem torments me so.

No. This is a monster. Why else would all of the many good things in my life not be enough?

Why else would the flickers of realization be pointing toward the underworld as the source of my tribulation?

Even if this monster gnaws and tears at my very soul, I hope it is a devil.

My discovery and defeat of the Sadist Psychologist and his Masochist Slut Sub is proof of my ability to overcome the power of devils.

I have no prior experience with Angels.

I have also had very little experience with indecision. AHA! An answer sprang into my mind. My problem is indecision!

I am having a tough time deciding to go back to my criminal method of providing for my family or of staying on the straight and narrow.

I really miss my less than legal life.

Don't question my yearning for I have no answer. My need is not based on poverty, lack of education, childhood abuse or any conventional excuse I can think of.

The desire exists. The targets are there. The knowledge is mine.

Put them all together and crimes <u>will be</u> all but committed.

The dark side is ascending. I need something to stop the craving.

It's time to don my thinking cap.

I can be a criminal, or I can be an officer of the law. How to chose? What are the real differences in working on the dark side and walking in the light?

The advantages of a life of crime are several.

What are the differences in Cops and Robbers?

As an independent crook;

You come and go, as you want to.

You answer to no boss.

You chose your own targets.

You plan your own jobs.

You alone are responsible for your success or failure.

You get to enjoy the thrill of the hunt when you're on a job searching for the loot.
You also enjoy a different, larger, thrill. It is the danger of the close encounter with capture if your plan is faulty.

As a Lawman;
Cops do not pick the job.
Cops stand less chance of living at San Quinton.
Cops don't always get the credit for a case they solve.
Cops don't earn as much if they stay honest.
Cops answer to a number of politicians.

None of these things really apply to private investigators. That's bad news for crime but good news for me.

I am Phantom, I play both sides against the middle and I'm inclined toward accepting a life of legitimacy.

With probable sporadic visits to the dark side.

I am wrong about one thing. My turmoil is not caused by indecision.

I just decided the kind of life to lead and the deep feeling of discontent remains. What then? What the hell is wrong?

It must be the absence of challenge.
Have I gotten lazy?

This is beginning to bug the crap out me.
How about you?
I think I'll give in and let the lazy way prevail.

I got a cup of coffee and turned on the television news in the hope that I could find something to take my mind in a different direction.

When I only need headlines the local radio and TV Anchorpersons do a fine job reading the gist of events.

A cursory explanation of what happened and where it happened is normally all television has so the item is gone in the next day's newscast.
An exception to the very sparse news coverage is their seemingly endless reading of catastrophes.

Day after day, all day, rehashing of mass murder, typhoons, and celebrity deaths no matter where in the world, or to whom, the event occurs.

Even the most trivial change, such as the make of a victim's car, will trigger the talking heads into a frenzy of repeating an already oft-stated story.

Of all things to engage my attention it was the story of a dog.

The anchor lady oooed and aaahed over the picture of what she said was a lost puppy.

The puppy looked so forlorn, sitting on the cement sidewalk in front of a two-story brick house. I couldn't help but be touched.

After breakfast I'm going to my office (the park) to flip a coin. Back to work I thought as I reached for the morning paper.

Out of town newspapers were appearing in my mailbox daily now.

Today, as a result of lax reporting, the paper's subscribers are fewer and the income from advertisers is diminishing.

To solve this problem and to be able to claim a wide readership, some of the printed media decided to mail free trials to people; whether or not the trials were requested.

Ergo, out of town newspapers are appearing in my mailbox.

Many newspapers, as few as they are becoming today, no longer keep to the traditions of carefully checking on, confirming and protecting sources.
Some editors no longer insist on double or triple checking information for factual accuracy.

At one time in-depth coverage by accredited journalists and resuming a case based on things like the make of a victim's car was only done if it was an important part of an important story.

Thank goodness there are still publishers that insist on their people adhering to the older, better standards.

These are the newspapers that provided me with targets away from my permanent location, which is a good thing. Remember one of life's lessons is "You don't shit where you eat."

# Chapter 23 Bow Wow

I left home for my office (the park) with a couple of area newspapers. When I was comfortable on a park bench my first act was to flip a coin. Heads for Cops, tails for Crime.

When I lifted my hand from the tossed-up nickel I saw the face of a president. Phantom Investigations will continue on the side of the righteous. Mostly.

I opened the Somerset Scribe in search of an interesting crime. I found some things of interest but not necessarily criminal.

Then my hand fell on the Boston Weekly Express, another of the ‘free trial’ papers, and guess the first story to greet me? The human-interest story on TV that caught my eye; the one about the “lost” puppy.

It was a nice coincidence, prompting me to read more regarding the lonely puppy.

The reporter, Jack Courtney assigned to cover this sort of news, did an excellent job.

The journalist got almost all of the important details right.

Scruffy, which is the puppy’s name is a male Jack Russell Terrier.

A fact Courtney included in his article further kindled my interest. The “lost” puppy was not lost. Scruffy lived at 4342 Casino Ave., the house in front of which the dog maintained the more or less constant lookout.

The two story brick dwelling was owned and occupied by Andrew Smyth, who it was said doted on his pet terrier, often taking the little dog to work with him.

Mr. Smyth disappeared two weeks ago. There was a missing person report given to the authorities, resulting in the usual next to nothing missing person's investigation.

The newspaper article said that friends and relatives of the homeowner took the puppy away every day or two, with no lasting result.

The small canine escapes their "rescue" only to return to what seems to be an extremely lonely vigil. It would appear that Scruffy is on stakeout waiting for his owner to return.

Mr. Smyth had offices in the Devils and Angels, a downtown club. This D&A was one of ten clubs strewn around the state that were owned by the Andrew Aggregate.

The buzzing of my cell phone disturbed my ruminations. It was Nora, my wife calling me to eat.

She prepared an outstanding Tuna Salad for dinner. This was an unusual treat, with walnuts, grapes and special seasonings made from Nora's Grandmother Rosie's recipe. Unexpected dishes like this were much appreciated by both Matt and myself. We expressed our pleasure several times during the meal in our usual table conversation.

It put a little damper on dinner when I explained that business would take me away from home for a little while again. Matt said he would take care of Mom. Nora said she would take care of Matt.

It was this sort of camaraderie that made me rue my increasingly often absences from home.

All the same, an easy correlation makes me well aware of the rewards garnered from the temporary loss of the family's companionship. I compare the house we now had to the coalmine shack we once lived in.

With my wife and son taking care of each other I knew all would be well without me, and packed for my sojourn to Bean Town.

Now that I'm settled in the Hotel Commerce, registered as Mark Darrow, I need to make up my mind if I'm going to look at this as Phantom, P.I. the Private Eye or as Phantom, M.D. the Master Desperado?

I decided to decide depending on where the puppy led me.

In any event I had to start somewhere so as usual I started at the end and drove my rented Ford to 4342 Casino Ave.

You are to smart for me.

# Chapter 24 Here doggie, doggie

You guessed that I was going to sit on the sidewalk with Scruffy and hope to gain some doggie details on the situation didn't you? You are right. I did, and I did.

The first thing the little pet told me is that Andrew always took him everywhere, except not this time. This time Smyth not only didn't take Scruffy with him, the dog was abandoned on the hot cement. No food, no water, no owner.

Furthermore the small canine seemed to like being where he was, returning to the same spot and circumstances even after being rescued by neighbors several times. I told myself to stop gathering the obvious data.

Scruffy is an intelligent pooch, like most of them are. He is trying to communicate some original knowledge to us.

Put it together. Dogs are known to wait in a certain place for their masters to return. They are also known to make grieving sounds for missing or deceased masters.

I've never known of one that was grieving, to make intermittently low growling sounds as if to ward off intruders.

Not until I met Scruffy on the sidewalk.

There are professional Long Jumpers and professional High Jumpers. Some might say I am a professional Conclusion Jumper. I play my hunches. Whatever you prefer to call it I am sure that now I know what the local police should have determined about the puppy.

The pet was trying to tell them that his master had been kidnapped.

The terrier is waiting for Smyth and for the thugs that took him.

Of course! The ones who took the dogs best friend <u>made</u> Andrew abandon his beloved Scruffy.

Why else would the pampered pooch not be scratching at the door of his home, or why not stay with the people who rescued him? Surely they would treat him well?

Why else would Scruffy return to the desolate, stark spot where he had been left alone? There is one hitch in this theory. Why did they snatch Smyth?

If his entire family consists of a Jack Russell Terrier how can the villains demand a ransom?

Scruffy can't answer the 'phone and he sure as hell can't read a fucking note.

Here's my first days score:

Questions? MANY

Answers? ONE GUESS.

## Chapter 25 Drawn In

Day two started after dinner when the night-lights come on and the nightlife comes out. My kind of people right now.

I was after some casual conversation at a few bars on a few street corners with a few drunks and a few whores to fill me in on the kind of man Smyth was.

It was often pointed out in the seamier quarters of the city that Adolph Hitler liked little dogs too, inferring that Smyth might not be what he purported to be.

More straight stuff bandied about in the shadowy streets of Bean Town was the name of Smyths' clubs.

Everyone knows, say the scoundrels, that Devil and Angel means Smyth and Honey.

None of the street people I contacted about Andrew Smyth had a good word for him, except for a few of the working girls.

That one-sided opinion of an apparently successful businessman opened the doors to a multitude of speculations.

My task is to accept the invitation, extended by my pure curiosity, to open the doors to truth.

I'll walk through those enticing portals of search and research, hoping to find the path I am to follow to the conclusion of the mystery that is now unearthed.

I have no choice. It is looking like I am the only one that gives a damn what happened to Andrew Smyth. Scruffy and I that is.

The small mutt has been by my side since I flew in to this strange city. When I give it any consideration, it stands out like a sore thumb that the Jack Russell is my single buddy in Boston.

Not just Buds but from now on we're Partners in this caper.

Now my new partner and I will search for someone, anyone, who will say anything nice about the owner of the Devils and Angels.

Where better to start than the D&A?

Andrew Smyth made the club his headquarters, so he spent a lot of time there, and must have interacted with many citizens in the course of doing business.

Added to that my partner knows the joint inside and out.

What the hell, Scruffy used to be there most days with Andrew so the dog probably knows the employees, and the steady customers as well.

Damn shame Scruffy can't talk. This would go a lot easier if he could.

My initial contact with the D&A girls was with a tall auburn haired beauty with amber eyes that were close to being chocolate brown.

Her first words to me were "Can I help you?"

I answered, "My name is Mark. Mark Darrow." I politely extended my hand to shake, which she paid no attention to.
"I'm an insurance salesman. I'd like to have an appointment with the owner of this establishment to discuss an insurance policy that will protect Devils & Angels from the claims of drunks.

Now you know who I am and what I want." I said politely, "May I ask your name and your position here?"

The Lady grinned, and her smile was in her eyes as well as on her lips. I liked her instantly.

"My name is Honey Potter, and I run this place when Andrew isn't here." were her words. After a half second of thought, her action was to offer her hand in welcome.

We shook hands gingerly but the smile never left her eyes.

Can you believe it is remotely possible to be true that Miss Potter was born with a name like Honey?

The lady swears it <u>is</u> the name on her birth certificate. She told me her father was a beekeeper named Potter and just couldn't resist the temptation to name his daughter Honey.

The minute we were in the club Scruffy made a beeline (no pun intended) in Honeys direction and jumped in her arms. (Bullshit the pun couldn't be ignored)

Honey hugged and kissed that Jack Russell as if he was Jack Kennedy and she was Marilyn Monroe.
Honey asked Scruffy where he had been, how he is, why he hadn't been around, if he had been sick, was he well, did he miss her, was he hungry, did he still love his Honey pot, and maybe six or seven more questions while she hugged him and rubbed his belly.

Miss Potter finally noticed I was still there. Clutching Scruffy to her breast the Lady said, "What the fuck were you doing with Scruffy? Where is Andrew?"

That's it two questions, two. One question considering she ran them together. Do you think she cared more about the pooch than she cared about me? Well, I guess that anyone Scruffy likes can't be all bad.

Honey continued holding Scruffy with one hand using her greeting hand to pet the dog with the other, while she glared at me and said "So?"

"I don't know Andrew or where he is. I found the mutt on a street corner. A friendly Cop told me it belongs to Andrew Smyth and to bring the little hound here. So I did, here we are." was my attempt at answering in kind. "If there is some kind of problem with Mr. Smyth I will be glad to help you in any way I can."

I was going to elaborate except the Lady broke in and interrupted my narrative with, "O.K. Mr. Mark Darrow, watch how you talk about this darling little puppy. His name is Scruffy, use it."

The not so sweet Honey said, “Scruffy is not a mutt or a hound. Scruffy is a pure bred Jack Russell Terrier. He deserves to be addressed by his name, Scruffy. Don’t you forget it.”

Miss Potter took a breath, scratched my partner between the ears and said to me, “I don’t know what the fuck you deserve yet. Tell me. What about this help?”

Honey must only have talked to me because I was Scruffy’s guest. No other reason comes to mind.

Nonetheless, having found the truth to be my best defense, as well as my best offense, I decided to lie to her. I told her that while I was making my insurance rounds I would keep an eye out for Mr. Smyth. I felt a small pang of regret that I lied to her, however it was way to early for the truth as yet. The facts will come if the time is right. If not, not.

To keep up the farce, of the insurance salesman that I was pretending to be until I came clean with Miss Potter, and needed more pertinent information; I asked some salesman questions. More relevant kinds of inquires may end in less than celebratory responses.

I spent my first week in town doing man-on-the street type interviews with bar-flies, sidewalk salesmen, working girls, snitches, panhandlers, the unemployed, the under employed, under-the-counter workers, and small time ‘Family’ members aching to get ‘made’.

These are what some of us call “people of the night”. I asked about Andy Smyth and the Devil & Angel.

This wide variety of dark-side citizens all shared a narrow, extremely narrow, opinion that Andrew Smyth was not a person you want to meet, particularly in a dark ally.

Many of the working girls had guarded compliments for Smyth. All others that we interviewed had nothing good to say about him.

When Andy’s name was omitted from questions about the Devils & Angels most of the people were nicer, saying things like, good food, good booze, good service, all-in-all a great place to enjoy a good time.

My plan was to conduct another seven days of man-on-the-street interviews. Thanks to Miss Potter I <u>could</u> skip this process by questioning her about her knowledge of Mr. Smyth if I chose to do so. How she feels about him is already obvious, I just needed to know why she feels that way.

I figured a week of interrogating a different stratum of society ought to balance the nightlife’s opinions. By doing these interviews around four thirty in the afternoon I should be talking to the kind of people who might stop in for a drink on the way home, or go to the D & A for dinner with the family. You know, just average Joe’s.

Of the residents I interviewed during the second sortie onto the streets of the city, nearly all of the middle class knew of the club.

The numbers showed that one out of four were patrons; half of them had met Andrew but didn't know him well enough to have an opinion.

The few who knew Smyth well enough to have a drink with him did not have a bad opinion of Andrew.
One of the most apparent things that jumps out of the two sets of interviews is that the underworld dislikes Smyth while the more respectable among us are neutral, tending to approve of Andy.

I found the dichotomy strange. Honey Potter did not. I had to know why she didn't.

Once again the information demands a quizzical stance. Time for Scruffy and me to revisit Miss Potter.

If anyone should know the good and the bad of her partner it is she. "Hi Honey" I said, "How are things at the D&A? Has our friend reappeared?" I said affably.
The lady was more disheartened than I have previously seen her.

The return to my query explained her despondence. "No. I haven't seen Andy, or heard anything from him for three weeks. Mark, I'm really worried about him.

In the five years we've been together this has never happened before. Andy has just vanished."

# Chapter 26 Honey Talks

Honey began to shed large tears. Even the presence of Scruffy in her lap couldn't stop the waterfall.

Understanding the situation entirely, I took no offense, when she looked at me with hateful eyes and said, "Where the hell is all this fucking help you promised you had for us?"

"Darlin' you don't know me, but you will soon enough. Trust me, I never break a promise." I promised. "Just to get things straight I don't sell insurance. I'm a private detective. I do need a little more enlightenment to get the lowdown on this assignment." I said.

"You lied to me," Honey said. "How can I trust you now?"

"You have my word that I will never lie to you again." I answered.

"Andy and I never lied to each other, and if you help me find him I will always be truthful with you too."

"In that case, you need to know that I sometimes operate outside of the law. Now you know all about me."

My initial attack on the mysterious disappearance was, "Why do scroungy people dislike Smyth and the D&A so much, while the cleaner crowd find them to be less than reprehensible?"

Honeys initial response was "Are you asking as the cop or as the crook?"

In accordance with our No More Lies agreement I could only tell the truth, "I have yet to make that determination for myself.  I will guarantee that either way your paramour will suffer as little as possible.  I reckon he will not suffer at all if I control the manner of his re-materialization."

Honey said, "So far your help hasn't been worth a damn, but you're the only game in town so I guess I'll take a seat."

Drying her eyes Honey told me what I had to know in order to save Andrew if he wasn't already dead.

"If you tell anyone what I am going to tell you now I'll cut off your balls and feed them to you like olives.  Do you understand?  Not one syllable!"

"Loud and clear" I agreed "Nothing to no one or you make my wife unhappy in the extreme."

"Regular folks only know Andy from the D&A. They don't know how he got it or what the place actually is." Honey started, "They think the Aggregate is simply a chain of pretty decent Bar & Grills, owned by a pretty decent man.

The general populace wouldn't believe the man I know."

" Come to think of it," Honey said with a faint smile on her lips "Andy is rather unbelievable, even for me."

Miss Potter took a breath and initiated her explanation.

"Andy and I were both outside the law when we first got together five years ago.
Neither one of us knew we were both dark, but I was a mule for the syndicate, he was a boss.

Now can you see why I demand that you keep your mouth shut?" Honey asked in a rather threatening voice.

"We happened to be on the same First Class Air International flight 707 to Rio one night and we struck up a conversation."

I introduced myself as Melinda Jefferson, on vacation for a few days.
He introduced himself as Juan Rojas, visiting his dying aunt.

The hours evaporated in the heat of our attraction for each other.
Love at First Sight is not a myth.

It is more like a terrible affliction.

I listened to him, talked to him, drank champagne with him and fell asleep with my head on his shoulder.

He slept with his arm around me, resting his beautiful face on the top of my black wig.

She said a rough landing in the country of the Gay Caballero awakened Juan and Melinda from an otherwise wonderfully smooth flight from Detroit.

Flight 707 landed with bumps and screeching tires; that bad landing was a forewarning of things to come.

Wanting to prolong the unexpected pleasure of the Rojas charm I suggested we enjoy our first Brazilia breakfast together. He accepted.

We consumed Pao Frances with sweet butter, papaya, queijo, and the strong dark coffee that Brazilia is world famous for.

Everything tasted much better here than the exact same meal would taste in the States.

The glitter of togetherness did not begin to fade.

We had sated our appetite, for food at least. Other unfulfilled propensities remained in the bellies of us both.

When the clock told us it was time for us to go our separate ways, I was certainly dejected thinking we could never appease our other hungers, and I am sure he was too, or so I imagined.

## Chapter 27 The Things Came

If we thought the Air International landing was rough, our next meeting is best described as cataclysmic.

Our second fortuitous encounter was behind Brazilia jail bars. I was stopped for a minor traffic violation. Juan was arrested on suspicion of theft.

Incarceration for trivialities and absolutely impossible suspicions may not occur often in North America, however here in Brazilia unjustified, possibly illegal, detentions were almost a daily event.

The upside to being falsely arrested, if there is an upside, was that we found ourselves locked in adjoining cells. This meant we could communicate with each other through the opening between the bars.

No sooner than my cell door slammed shut with a loud clash, Senor Rojas was trying to calm my nerves.

Juan looked me in the eye and said, "Don't be alarmed, Melinda. You are innocent of any wrongdoing. We just arrived in their country; these kinds of counterfeit charges against tourists usually come as a cover for much worse crimes that the policia want time to find evidence of.

Before I go on, he went on, Rojas told me he wanted me to know that he wished to extend our relationship once we're back home."

Juan also said he didn't want the Genie of honesty to jump out of a lamp and kill the chance of his wish coming true. He paused, and then he said, "With my following confession, and your authentic answers to my questions, there may be a way we can get out of this jail alive."

I wanted him to continue, but I practically begged Juan to please not let the Genie kill my dream either. I too wanted to extend whatever we had together.

Nevertheless, I told Juan I wanted us to be honest with each other, so if my dream became our dream it would be strong enough to weather any storm we were caught in.

He said for me to prepare to batten down the hatches.

"Melinda." he said, "My name is not Juan Rojas."

Suddenly the door to the cell block was thrown open again and what appeared to be a laundry bag stained with blood was thrown on the floor in front of Andy's enclosure. The bag groaned once then was silent.

I was startled and started to rise to see what they threw at us. Juan, or whoever he was, waved his hand in front of my face and told me to wait.

He said whatever was in that bag may well be dead, or dying.

Rojas wanted me to let him finish what he had to say.

That's when he told me his name is Andrew Smyth and there is no dying aunt.

## Chapter 28 El Presidente

Andy also told me he was a Boss in the Family, down here on a buying trip. He said our jailors were after the half a million dollars in cash Andy brought with him.

When the newly re-named Mr. Smyth quit confessing his pretense, he demanded that I tell my story.

Andrew said he knew I didn't come down here to vacation. He was right. I was not on vacation. Just the opposite, I was also at work.

I too confessed to using an alias. I told him my real name.

You quit grinning, my name really is Honey Potter.

This is the long explanation you asked me for so don't distract me.

To get on with it I know I must have looked at him with squinted eyes when I told him that I'd heard his real name before.

You're my boss I told him, or one of them. We never met but I certainly heard your name. You see the Family is paying me too. I'm what you guys call a 'mule'.

At that his eyes went wide and Andy said we were meant to meet. He explained that I was the one that was supposed to pick up the drop for him.

We both laughed. There is a saying "What a load of shit." I am pretty sure you have heard Narcotics are frequently called "shit".

My package was going to be left at Excelsior Hotel lobby in the last booth in the MEN'S ROOM.

Our mirth was short-lived the moment it struck us that our jobs had to be Hush-Hush.

There was only one way our mission could be brought to the light. That was by a snitch in the pipeline!

Our mission was to buy from the Little Man (Guzmahn) organization. Little Man ran the single largest drug cartel in the world.

It was un-thinkable that he would be betray us for any reason.

However it was entirely possible that the rat who is informing on us is not someone trying to hurt us; it is someone trying to destroy Guzmahn. .

Hard as we tried, no one came to mind that we thought would turn us in, with one unlikely, just possible scenario.

That snitch could be Viper. The Snake's the only person we can come up with that might have a motive to see a half million dollar buy go bad.

No matter how hard we tried no other name came to mind. As we said, it was unlikely, but possible. The real name of Snake was Allen (The Viper) Clark. Why on earth did it seem possible that The Viper would sabotage Guzmahn?

Little Man is the overlord of the underworld. The Viper is the second largest drug dealer in Brazilia.

## Chapter 29 Take a Message

Guzmahn is the Numero Uno kingpin of the drug world.

Maybe Snake wanted to take a giant leap to become number one himself?

Our ruminations came to an abrupt stop when the bloody laundry bag moved.

Whatever moved inside that bag hadn't died yet. It made another noise. That noise turned out not only to be the sound leading to of our freedom; it was also the announcement of our prosperity.

Andrew reached through the bars and untied the bloody bag, to release the bleeding animal dying inside. He managed to turn it 'til the closed end was facing us. We each took a corner of the cloth and stood up.

Andy and I picked up the bag by the bottom corners to shake out the contents

Mark, we thought a small lamb fell out. Until the lamb spoke.

The dying animal transformed into a naked, broken, beaten, and bleeding body of a dying boy. The young man must have been clinging to life by a single vein that miraculously escaped damage from the hundreds of blows inflicted by a thin hard rod of some sort.

The door to the cellblock re-opened, this time for the sweating figure of a female holding a long thin rod. The blood drying on her arms and on the rod she held, left little doubt as to her recent activities.

Andrew made many trips to Brazilia so the woman was not unknown to him.

It was Halle Hernandez, the president of the Federative Republic of Brazilia.

"How in Gods' name, I wondered", Honey said to me, "can we be called the gentler sex."

Standing beside Her Excellency was a bespecled elderly man. A soldier toting a machine-gun stood guard.

La Presidente turned to the old man beside her saying she beat the boy within an inch of his life and would have taken the last inch but she wanted to send a message to the cocksucking father of the little son-of-a-bitch.

She told the man, apparently a physician; to get the little puke back on his feet, then send him home along with this stupid bastard, she said, pointing to Andrew, who entered her country illegally to buy Little Mans shit. This presidential bitch approached Andrew within an arms length, still wielding the thin, bloody rod in her hand.

President Hernandez called Andy a stupid fucking idiot, and told him the reason she was letting him live was so he could be her delivery boy.

The disheveled woman said she hoped Andrew had brains enough to get this message right. "Tell that retarded piece of shit you work for, that he may be a big time dope dealer, that thinks he owns this country, but I own Brazilia.
I'm not afraid of him or of any filth like him.

To prove Brazilia belongs to me I am going to run his ass out of my nation."

This terrible female also said to Andy, "Take your nose out of Guzmahn's stinking asshole long enough to tell him exactly what I just said. Can you do that? I hope so," she added, "because here's just a taste of what I'll give your whore if you get it wrong." Lightening fast the rod struck Andy's face. The cut was deep enough to leave the scar he carries on his right cheek to this day. My Decision to kill the bitch hardened."

Honey stopped her narrative to dab at her eyes and to question me. "Well Mark it's your turn. Will you talk for a few minutes? I'm running down."

"I can see these memories are painful for you," I said, "Name a subject and I'll expound on it to give you a short relief." I offered. Honey gave me a look full of predetermined answers.

Speaking with the faint smile I am becoming accustomed to, Honey said, "Talk Truth to me now. Give me your honest assessment of the Rio couple."

## Chapter 30 True of False

I dove right in saying, “If you did not postulate Truth I could craft a more flattering point of view. In as much as you demand the nitty-gritty you may want a drink to make things more palatable”

“Oh no” said Honey “I think you’re on the right track, for this part of the race that is.”

“Go on.” she urged “Let me discover your detecting powers, how well you follow the clues to a correct conclusion.”

“Then pour me a double scotch, neat.” I ordered. “My perception of both of you is negative to state it as politely as I am able to, and remain within the boundary you yourself described.

You say you were a ‘Mule’ and your companion was a Boss.

That means each of you were knowingly working for, and being paid by, and following the instructions of, an organization that is openly operating beyond the law.

It was, and still is, a gang that controls, or has a large share in controlling, the semi accepted trades of Bets, Broads, & Booze (gambling, prostitution, and alcohol).

These people, known as The Mob, The Company, The Cosa Nostra, and locally as The Family, are also connected to shipping, construction, sanitation and other businesses. Some legal, some not.

The two of you were on the particularly evil leg of the beast. You participated in the part of the business that automatically destroyed lives.
Each of you, individually, chose to deal in narcotics.
You knew, or at least Smyth did, that once the needle pierced the skin, the soul left the body through that tiny puncture.

Preposterous isn't it that the evil substance was injected into the bloodstream of the addicted with an instrument invented to save lives.

I think so.

Isn't it also Ironic that for a meager stipend you and Andy provided a product that only brings relentless misery to men, women, or children, who were in the vain search for happiness?
Honey, you have a name as sweet as sugar, but you must have or at one time had, morals as bitter as your first lost love.

Tell me Miss Potter what inducement is there that is worth acting as a pack animal?
You let yourself become a mule, bringing a life of degradation to newborn addicts, Hard Babies, born craving dope.
Newborns, whose pregnant mothers had an addiction that made them love shooting heroin even more than they loved the fetus they were carrying.

Maybe there are enough dollars to justify turning a teenage child into a filthy do-anything-for-a-fix whore.

I don't think I can count that high.

It is also obvious that the cold hard cash was hard enough and cold enough to block your sense of pity; An emotion you should have felt for the men now shooting up who will sacrifice wives, kids, well paying jobs, anything at all for the devil of dope.

The first time they tightened a rubber tube around their arm looking for a place to inject the stuff some mule brought up from the south; every one of them lost, or will lose, everything they had, or ever could have had."

Honey was crying, sobbing, in clear distress.

When I quit talking she blubbered out "I didn't think! I wasn't selling drugs. I just delivered packages.

I thought it was like delivering liquor during prohibition.
Something recreational that people liked and is legal now.

Oh My Lord! I didn't think! How many have I hurt! God please forgive me. I just didn't realize what I was doing." Her voice faded out, the tears continued for a while longer.

I sat in silence, knowing that what I said was true, still I felt regret for hurting her.

Scruffy whined and kissed her face trying to lick away the sorrow.

I continued doing as I was asked to do i.e. telling her the truth about what I garnered from her original meeting with Mr. Smyth.

"Honey you were not alone in your infamy. Not when you were in Brazilia, and not before. You were but a very small cog in the drug machine you helped maintain.

Andrew on the other hand was a much bigger wheel, thus vastly more responsible. He did know what he was doing, since he was once stuck in the muck personally.

Part of my investigation the couple of weeks prior to my meeting with Honey uncovered interesting information concerning the Devil & Angel owner's youth.

At one time, when Andrew Smyth was seventeen he was the star of his schools soccer team. According to another one of the members on the soccer team, Oral Blankenship, they won the state championship that year only because Smyth headed the winning ball into the net.

Coach Farnsworthy wanted to reward his star athlete, so he called Andy into the office, shut and locked the door, and pulled the blind closed.

Coach laughed when he saw Andy getting nervous and told him to relax this meeting was for fun.

When coach pulled a hundred dollar bill out of his pocket Andy jumped to the wrong idea again and got up to leave.
Coach laughed again and told Smyth to sit down and watch. Farnsworthy took a vial from his pocket, and then poured a white powder out of the vial onto the desk. Coach picked up an index card and used it to shape the powder into four separate lines.

Rolling the bill into a hundred-dollar straw Coached used the tube to sniff up two of the lines of powder, one line in each nostril. Then he handed the rolled up bill to Andy saying "the money is my way of saying thanks for the great plays tonight. So is the snow."

Coach knew Andy didn't do drugs so he urged, "go on kid try it once, it won't hurt you and you'll love it. This stuff is as good as sex ever was.

Smyth took the rolled up bill, sniffed up the two white lines, and was hooked.

I asked Oral how he knew all this? Was he in the office too? "Easy," he said, "Andy told me all about it when he wanted me to try some. Free. You see Andy did try it once when Coach told him to and a hundred times after since it was so good."

I asked Blankenship if he accepted. "Hell no," he replied, I knew Andy was giving it away the first time. After you were addicted to it he got whatever he wanted for the stuff you craved and you did actually crave the shit."

"No Honey," I said, "you were not alone. Your boyfriend may be charming now, but he sure as fuck is no Angel. He knows without question that once addicted you literally go through hell to escape the prison of dope. Most junkies never find their way out. Many die trying. The Devil in Devils & Angels was stronger than most and Luckier than shit.

None of which ameliorates this fact; If not now, at one time you and Andrew Smyth both dealt in drugs.

How many infants do you think could suckle at the teat of the half million dollars worth of cocaine you were to deliver?

I am beginning to see why so many people hate the Boss. They would also despise the Mule if they knew of your reason for going to Brazilia"

Honey stifled her sobs, wiped her eyes, and said, "I cannot alter a single moment of my past no matter how long I cry, and my future is not assured, no matter how much I pray.

This is all I have, this minute that I live.

I resolve to do my best to atone for my earlier mistakes, and as long as I am here I will do all I can to help others make it through this little time we have on earth.

Honey blew her nose and resumed her story.

# Chapter 31 In a Gilded

"We have already learned the lovely lady politician did not forego threats, or torture, and likely even murder to reach her goals. This gruesome lesson fell out of that bloody bag with the nearly butchered body of Little Mans son.

It will come as no surprise then that the bitch exhibited no remorse when she ordered me kidnapped and held naked in a cage for all to see.

It was this less then pretty picture presented to Andy when he was brought into the room where my cage swung from the rafters.

Discarding any pretense of modesty I pressed myself against the bars of the cage attempting to get as close to him as possible.

Refusing to allow the handcuffs and leg-irons that bound him to keep Andy from me he charged the cage, only to stumble awkwardly.

To keep from falling Andrew grabbed the bars that I was holding on to. I was astonished to see a crooked smile on his mouth as his face slammed into the bars.

Nevertheless, my heart rejoiced when my ears heard the whispered words "Don't give up," he also whispered, "I'll get you out soon" and "I'm going to kill that cunt."

That horrible thin rod clanged against the bars of the cage near my face. The bitch told us that conjugal visiting time was over.

Her cackled cacophony indicating that she imagined the remark to be hilarious.

I made an involuntary cry as she signaled two guards to take the prisoner away. Tears ran in rivulets through the dirt on my cheeks as they dragged my shackled man out of the enclosure.

The massive doors slowly closed while the horrendous harlot laughed her crazy cackle.

I did not see, hear, or get word of the man I fell in love with, for several days. Still I never gave up, constantly remembering his parting words, "I'll get you out soon."

It was a lot like what's happening now.

Yet even in those deadly days my heart reached out to Andy and I felt the warmth of his love return. Can you understand my current fear?"

"Yes, Honey I can." I replied. I was thinking of Nora and our son.

Andrew Smyth, Family Boss, man of power, wielder of fear and large amounts of cash was sitting in front of the desk of Brazilas Chief Executive.

He was listening to a rehash of the instructions she had given him earlier.

Always mindful of my feelings Andy waited 'till we knew each other better to tell me this part of his dealings with the modern Medusa.

We know each other much better now, in fact I heard about this in his bed.
She told Andy of the loathsome consequences that would befall me if he failed in his assignment.

I won't delve into the disgusting details of her intentions.

Andrew owns an awe-inspiring confidence.
No doubt a talent he earned in his struggle with coke when he was younger.
He was confident, but not crazy, so this Family man clothed himself in the camouflage of submission.
Andrew told me that he used his most domesticated persona to plead for her not to harm me.
He promised in his most servile voice to do as she commanded.
Andrew got down on his knees and begged for my release when the deed was done.

I'm glad I didn't have to witness his Oscar winning performance.
I could hardly believe this upper echelon member of the Family would debase himself for any reason and I told him so.
Andrews's answer thrilled me. He said, "That's because you've never been in love."
Little did he know I was <u>looking</u> at my love.
My soul mate Andy, told me he became a piece of Humble Pie, and like good pie she ate it up.

## Chapter 32 Presidential Interview

The bitch forgot that too much of a good thing can kill you.

Andy's aspiration was to jog her memory.

Andrew told me that he used his most defeated persona to plead for her not to harm me. He promised in his most subdued voice to do as she commanded.

The whore woman simply put her foot against his shoulder and pushed him to the floor.

"Get out of here you sniveling coward. Deliver Guzmahn's kid with my message and I promise to let you both return to the States unharmed."

Of course she was lying through her teeth. She knew it. Andy knew it.

There was one little thing she didn't know but would soon learn.

Andy told me that after his unsavory clash with the witch he and the boy were driven to the center of the town's shoddiest neighborhood. There the limo stopped and the two of them were practically thrown from the car.

As the automobile bearing the presidential seal sped off, a dirty, disheveled old man clutching a brown paper bag hobbled up to Andy.

The old guy appeared to be your typical wino with a bottle of Boons Farm, or some other cheap wine, in the bag.

This bum proved to be anything but a drunk and instead of a bottle of Boons, there was a Mauser in the bag pointed directly at him.

The geezer asked Smyth his name and what state he was in. Andy said he told the bum his Family Password; “My name is Angel and I live in the state of grace.”

It struck me as a bit sacrilegious for a bunch of crooks to use such a password. It kinda pissed me off too, ‘cause I was never told we even had a fucking password.

I guess mules are more expendable than I wanted to believe.

Honey got back on track. The odd little fellow cracked a snaggle toothed smile and called Andy by name. The ersatz drunk said he was happy to meet Mr. Smyth.

The Boons Farmer said he was glad to see him still walkin’ and talkin’.

Now Andy was Mr. Smyth again, not “worthless piece of shit” like the presidential pussy named him.

Andy and the boy were then taken to a Mercedes Benz parked around the corner waiting for him.

Andy said he was driven to an abandoned warehouse the city owned but never used.

As the garage doors closed behind the car, a large entrance to a well-lighted tunnel opened in the floor. Andrew said he met this revelation with a smile that Little Man was at it again, digging escape routes.
The difference with this one is it appeared to be quite an elaborate entrance not just a mole hole in the ground.

This tunnel was so well finished it could provide a speedy way out of wherever the drug lord was.

They rode for almost five minutes ‘till they came to a stop. The tunnel ended on a turntable. The driver cut the engine of the vehicle and the platform turned to align the passenger side of the MB with a set of four doors.

The portal on the far left opened and a friend of Andrew’s emerged. The chauffer opened the door for Andy then offered his hand to Omar, as the child had identified himself to us.

Andrew said Manny Guzmahn did not greet him with the usual good cheer Little Man had exhibited at all of their other meetings during the fourteen years they had known each other.

Little Man ignored me, Andy said, and instead took his injured son in his arms, telling the boy that he would recover and he would be avenged.

Not until the driver took charge of Omar, did Manny turn to Smyth.

Aside from the fact that the kid had suffered a terrible beating; everything else was to be thankful for; no missing appendages, his son's eyes remained undamaged and the child was lucid. None of which will be true of La Presidente when she pays the debt she now owes Omar.

A fierce look covered Little Man's face in spite of the grateful words of relief that his son was intact.

Andy told me of the talk he had with Little Man when things had returned to a more normal footing.

Andrew said to Little Man that they've done business for almost fifteen years and been friends for five, right? "Si amigo," replied the Boss of Blow, "Much business, but the many mutual interests are the reason for the friendship."

Guzmahn wanted to know the reason for the question.

Andrew said he told Manny the cause of his unease was simple. Andy said in all these years there had been no mention of a son or of any children. Most men brag about their offspring 'till it gets boring. You never brag to me. Why not?

The next thing that happened was more than astonishing inasmuch as the drug lord was reputed to be the meanest son-of-a-bitch to walk the face of this earth.

Still wearing the Wrath of God on his countenance Manny (Little Man) Guzmahn started to cry.

## Chapter 33 Plan Gone Wrong

Wiping his eyes the grief stricken man told Andrew that no one knew Omar was his son.
Not even his brother.
Guzmahn told Andrew he wanted his son to be anonymous.

Little Man saw to it that Omar and his mother lived fairly well in one of the upper level homes in the compound. The boy went to the same school as the other kids, played ball with his friends, and was as normal as possible.
It was an obviously failed effort to keep the kid safe.

Mannys tears disappeared, but the wrath remained when he said only one other person knew the truth, Omar's mother.
Little Man said I'm going to kill the bitch for betraying my boy. Then I'm going after La Presidente. She will die a hundred times over, knowing what real torture is, for what she did to my son.

Andy told me that this is when he inadvertently made a life changing decision.

One of the commonalities Manny and he shared was the deep-seated belief that they should assist their friends in every possible way, and defeat their adversaries without mercy.

Andy came to the determination to kill two birds with one stone.

Little Man was his friend and la Presidente was his enemy. Ergo, Andrew thought, "I will help my friend fight our enemy."

The best way possible to help his friend was to keep Manny from wantonly murdering Omar's mother.

Andrew knew that Little Man was of more than average intelligence and would listen to a reasonable argument. For that reason Andy said he first explained to Manny why he would help to bring down the murderous bitch that tortured Omar, and the person who fingered Omar in the first place.

Andy also told Little Man that he had a plan to do it and to get away with it.

A way Guzmahn would enjoy his full ruthlessness without endangering his domain under any circumstance.

Andy said this statement enticed the afflicted man who said, "Speak Smyth. Say your say then go find us something to drink while I think".

Andy left the room as requested, after telling the Deacon of Dope he had been hatching the plan since the minute Andy and I had been arrested.

Andrew told me he walked around the compound for about thirty minutes to give Little Man a chance to think, before taking two large mugs of coffee back to the room.

Andy told Honey that when he returned with the Joe, he wanted to lighten up the coming discussion.

Andrew entered saying "Here ya go Manny. Just like you like your women."

The ploy to bring a little levity in with the drinks must be working for Little Man replied with "black, hot, and sweet?"

Then Andy told me they got down to where the rubber met the road. Andrew was told to "Spit it out. How can we do what is necessary and escape unscathed?"

Manny slipped out of the mournful mode into the full-blown Little Man personality.
The mastermind that built an international empire on the weakness of distraught humans all over the world, once again became a Drug Lord.
No, not A drug lord.

Manny became THE Drug Lord whose mere nod could literally make a strong man piss his pants. Manny no longer existed.

In this reincarnation of himself butchery was beautiful. Guzmahn had become one hundred percent an entity of Vengeance. He was entirely Little Man.

The first unpalatable piece of the plan was to attempt to deprive the Lord of Laudanum the satisfaction he could attain from the murdering Omar's mother; the woman he knocked-up for the sole reason that he might sire a son.

You won't like this Andy said he told Little Man. " The number one necessity is to leave Omar's mother alone for now." After Little Man settled down and was ready to listen to logic Andrew carried on. Andy said he would visit Omar and while there he would pump mama for information about how she thought word got out on her child's lineage.

Andrew said he was of the opinion that the cartel interviewed enough people to know that when the guilty were led to believe they were not suspected, and they were treated as an innocent, you were odds-on to win usefully accurate news from them.

Andy then said he pointed out that killing Omar's mother might quell Manny's quest for retribution; but the unending damage to his son such an action would precipitate, would far outdo any pain inflicted on the boy by the political whore.

This part of Andrews recount of his meeting with Little Man would have ended if these stipulations were not accepted.

Andy told me that he could feel a question about to escape Manny's mouth that might end this coffee get together and more.

The look on the Master of Murders face indicated that the answer to this single question might destroy nearly fifteen years of symbiosis.

Andrew said the question came in a slow, low, measured, mean tinged voice. It was a simple query, requiring a complex answer.
Little Man issued a one-word inquisition. He asked, "When?"

Andy was correct in his trepidation. There was no smile on Little Mans face. There was no light in his eyes.

Little Man was in his most dangerous mood.

With his answer, Andy set the course to the ultimate demise of Brazilia's President.
"When Omar is protected and his tormentor is in your tender care."

Andy reported his great relief when the response satisfied the desire for blood Little Man was feeling at the moment.

Answers to other questions, he said would rule the safe or not safe culmination of the impending unadulterated retaliation.

This time there was no menace behind the next one-word question, which was, How?
This reply would be more complicated also would take longer.

Andrew let me know the involved plan he outlined for the mourning father.
In its' essence though the plan was a simple (?) kidnapping of the President of a large nation.

## Chapter 34 A Golden Gift

When the scheme was approved Andy asked Manny if he had any curare?

"Little Man asked How much do you need? Who and how many do you intend to murder?" Phase one of what the co-conspirators named Operation Recall got underway.

As the plan unfolded it was crystal clear that they might get only half of what they wanted. It was possible too they would accomplish nothing if they didn't move quickly.

Honey found it hard to swallow that the first action was designed to rescue her from the grasp of the Nightmare Queen.

To snatch Honey from the clutches of sure death Andrew used the "Carrot and The Stick" approach. It was a method Andy said he was positive some version of which was S.O.P. for the Guzmahn Cartel.

The tried and true "Do or Die's" singular success was due to its extreme simplicity; Do as I want and I'll make you rich, don't do as I want and I'll make you dead. Simple, succinct, and scary as hell.

Also living <u>in</u> clover or sleeping <u>under</u> the clover is normally an easy choice.

A limousine driver and six heavily armed guards were in charge of my confinement. All of them were offered the Do or Die contract.

The individual guards earned one million dollars each and safe transportation to anywhere in the world that they wished to call home.

The chauffer was offered two million dollars with the same safety provisions. He was made Captain of the group. It was his duty to see to it that there were no glitches in the game.

The cartel spent seven million dollars to secure Honey's escape from hell. The price would have been even higher if Roberto, one of the guards, had not refused the money.

It was beyond his belief that anyone would pay him a million dollars for anything.

The lone refusal in the group also came because that guard knew in his heart that no one could break into the inescapable confines in which he worked, to kill him. Besides Roberto was surrounded by five of his brothers-in-arms, each of them carried an assortment of weapons. Ha! He thought the cartel couldn't kill me, even if they wanted to.

They wanted to, and they did.

Roberto suffered minimum pain as a stiletto punctured the back of his neck to sever vertebrae thus separating his brain from his body.

"Adios Amigo", one of his friends said, as he wiped blood from his dagger and returned the blade to its' scabbard.

The soldier left the corpse of his brother-in-arms to enter it's eternal sleep on a filthy prison floor.

# Chapter 35 How

Honey went on with her explanation of events by saying, "I was sedated. I was taken to the prison mortuary after the cartels' Doctor, who had never seen me let-alone made an examination of the 'deceased', signed my death certificate.

The prison Doctor, who had long been on the cartel payroll to take extra care of their incarcerated members, pronounced me dead of a heart attack.

From the dead room they spirited me away through one of several long forgotten escape tunnels.

Tunnels long forgotten by everyone except Little Man, the Emperor of Escapes.

Upon arrival in Mannys' compound Little Man ordered me taken to the infirmary where Senora Maria Gonzales, M.D. was assigned to my case twenty four seven.

Andrew sat by my side every available minute. I awoke from the sedation three days later to feel my hand being held by Andy.

He caressed my lips with his as soon as my eyelids fluttered. The dream we both desired was alive and well.

Little Mans' dream was, as yet, unfulfilled.

Phase Two of Operation Recall will let Manny rest <u>his</u> head on the pillow of revenge.

This part of the plan called for the Americano to once again prostrate himself at the feet of the nations premier bitch.

It also called for Andrew to risk instant death by her hand.

The soon-to-be Devil of the Devils & Angels willingly risked his life as small payment to Little Man for the survival of Honey.

Andy thought of it as a minor risk for a major reward. Whatever happened to him, the Rio cunt would die and Manny would be avenged.

Andy went back to the same street where the presidential chauffeur put him out of the limo two days ago. Someone must have informed the capitol of Andrews's appearance in the hood.

Minutes after his arrival a long black Mercedes stopped in front of Smyth. He was ordered to get in.

When the door of the limousine opened again, to let him exit at the capitol, Andy's first thought was 'thank God I'm still alive'.

Andrew was roughly shoved into the presence of the president and he instantly began his servile attitude.

With his most wheedling voice, Andy told the whore he brought her good news.

"Well spit it out. Don't just grovel there like the idiot you are!" the Rut of Rio growled.

"Please Madam," begged the guy who would shortly be the death of her, "let me see Honey."

Pretending to want to please her he added, "I brought you a gift. I risked a painful death to steal this from the bastard after I delivered your message. "May I see her now?" he whined.

La Presidente, thought the girl died of a heart attack yesterday.

For a very brief moment she considered telling him the truth; but like all of those moments of honesty this one also evaporated in a split-second and she said, "Of course you can. I gave you my word didn't I? Now show me what you have for me."

Without saying anything more I reached into my pocket and produced a beautiful star shaped gold broach.

Like the greedy shit I knew she was the President grabbed the golden star in my hand. "Ouch" she cried, "I stuck myself with the dammed thing."

Remember the request for curare?

The tip of each point of the beautiful golden star, as well as the pin on the clasp was treated with minute amounts of the poison.
Not enough to kill her, but plenty to affect her musculature after a minute or so and cause her to collapse.

The Presidents permanent guard watched it all.

The guard called for help to get the woman's unconscious body into an ambulance to be taken to the national hospital.

Help was Johnny on the spot. Medics were in the room to give assistance within seconds. So was the Vice President.

He questioned the Presidents guard about what occurred. The V.P. was told that she just fainted. The guard was positive I didn't do anything to harm her.

Since the President was in conference with me at the time of her mishap I was told to stay with the medics to give them any information I could about her collapse.

The E.M.T.'s applied plasma bags, loaded her on a gurney, and away we went toward the national medical center, transporting the nations leader to her kismet.

The President had been recalled.

We have all known for many years about "The long arm of the law", but we never hear about "The Spidery Reach of the cartels", which has been around, discretely, for many more decades than the "Long Arm."

The extensive worldwide webs the cartels weave are made of money. Their webs snare prey both large and small. The personnel of the ambulance transporting the horrible whore, Halle Hernandez, were among the people lured by money into the inescapable trap of greed.

She was no longer a President, now Halle was only a Prisoner.

# Chapter 36 Noel

Three miles short of the purported destination of the ambulance the vehicle swerved off the road and crossed the berm.
We were headed straight toward two tall pine trees, and the driver didn't slow down or even try to brake.

I grabbed hold of the gurney and swore the ambulance must be out of control, and a crash was unavoidable, we were going to wreck.

Magically the evergreens parted like the swinging doors of a gaucho's saloon.
When we safely passed through those swinging conifers I knew I just opened the best Christmas present of my life. I was just given my life

The unfazed driver was on an apparently seldom-used dirt roadway. We were now on course to the true destination of the E.M.T.'s medical bus. Little Man and Andrew waited at Manny's compound, where the detour ended.

That this once queenly beauty's limp body was pushed unceremoniously from the rear of the ambulance was as it should be. Since Halle, her satanic self was emitted from the rear, she landed on a pile of goat shit in the dusty square of the compound.

Little Man was true to his word.
The person who tortured his son would pay a thousand times for that transgression.
Halle was hung splayed, by her ankles, naked and used as an ashtray by his troops for three hours a day.

The other twenty-one hours every day she was kept bare and chained to a post outside in the courtyard.

Halle was fed a small piece of bread, a couple of ounces of cheese and half a cup of water once a day. Not enough to live on very long.
However she would live just long enough to stretch her torment out a few more weeks.

Andrews's debt to Manny was paid in full.

I have often wondered how a man that would extract such horrible vengeance on his enemies could do what the drug lord did next.

Honey said she recovered quickly with Andrew's loving ever-present help, and Manny's magnificent medical staff.
Miss Potter and her inamorata were packing to return to the States, when Little Man asked Andrew to sit out in the shade and have a last cup of coffee with him.

The two left for the porch, and a cup of real Colombian brew, a private conversation, and life-changing decisions for hundreds of people.
Maybe even thousands of people before this dance is over.

The following may not be verbatim but it is the gist of the conversation according to what a surprised and thankful Andy told Honey.

When the two men had been served their caffeine Little Man initiated the discourse with the somewhat disturbing statement.

Guzmahn said that he believed in people paying for the favors they get. Andy interrupted, saying "Come on Manny, I paid my dues.

You have the bitch strung up in the courtyard. I delivered," Andy was in turn interrupted.

Little Man said "Me Andy, not you. Me. I am the one with the priceless favor to repay and Andy, you hold the paper, in a manner of speaking. That is why I asked you to have coffee with me this morning."

"Wait a minute," Andrew joked "are you trying to settle some imaginary priceless debt to me with a cup of coffee? Must be damned good coffee."

"It is Andy, the blend is truly delicious. Nevertheless the I.O.U. is not imaginary, and coffee is not the payment.

Because of you there is joy in my life again. My son is alive and recovering. Omar is able to walk again; he's talking, even laughing again. Don't you call such a gift priceless?"

Manny continued, "It is all because of <u>you</u> and <u>your plan</u> that the cunt that tortured my boy to the point of death, now knows what he went through and she will never hurt him again.

You gave everything you had; your money, your dignity, and your position with the Family. You risked your health, your freedom and your wealth.
You even offered your life for the return of my son.

I call that priceless. I consider it to be an obligation hard to satisfy."

Andrew said "As far as I am concerned Manny we are dead even. We, not I, We saved Honey and We saved Omar and We brought the President to justice.

We should thank each other and stamp this enterprise paid-in-full."

"I agree." said Little Man, " When you brought my son back, when my little boy was returned home, I marked you up paid-in-full now and in the future.

I will never forget what you did. You risked all you are or could ever become, to save my Omar. That fact diminishes my small repayment installment by light years."

At the conclusion of his speech Little Man handed Andrew a beautiful blood red silk bag.

The bag contained fourteen pounds of variously cut blue-white diamonds.
Later we would find that the smallest of them appraised at one carat.

Pushing the bag full of gems back across the table to little man Andrew said, "this is overly generous but I can't let you do this. I did what I did for Honey as well as for Omar."

"Overly generous?" Replied Manny "I think it's pitifully small.
My business is worldwide and nets several billion dollars every few months.
Those rocks were all the goodies I have on hand, but a forever line of non-repayment credit with my banks is another installment on my note with you."

"O.K. Manny O.K., I've known you for some time now, and I know you love and take care of all of your people, but what is this?" questioned Andrew. He continued "This not something even a fiction writer would allow you to do."

Manny laughed at that and said "Writers can kiss my rosy ass. They usually don't have a clue of real life motivations."
"But" objected Andy "They do know that those of us in the drug trade are only motivated by the money. They do know that we cause people to become addicts and ruin themselves."

"So?" asked, the drug Lord "We are in it for the money," he agreed, " In spite of that, we do not cause addiction or ruin lives like some billionaire "investors" do. They make stock prices fluctuate in a manner that suits themselves, knowing full well that all of the small investors in those stocks will be ruined.
Will the people or their governments close the markets? Very rarely. Only in the most flagrant cases is anyone even tried in a court of law.

We do provide products that some people become addicted to," Little Man argued,

"So do producers of things like the Korean rotgut vodka, Jinro Soju, which sold 61 million cases of their hooch last year, or prescriptions for stuff like Humira which sells more than ten billion dollars worth a year, or even Keurig coffee. They bring in over two billion dollars a year. There are hundreds of other companies producing potentially addictive products and cashing large checks every year.

Do the writers think those guys are in it for the exercise? Hell no they're not! They want the profits, as do the thousands of 'respectable' stockholders buying shares in these possibly ruinous products.

Do you think the states that legalize, and own, the sale of alcohol give a shit if their customers become addicted?

Hell no, it just means alcoholics drink a lot more, and buy more booze.

Why are dangerous drugs like tobacco and alcohol legal? The answer to this question is really simple. They are legal because people want them and because the government is the Pusher, reaping huge profits from those addictive products in the form of taxes.

Odds are your congressman is in politics for the money and power, and is a likely user of rotgut too!"

The drug Lord continued, “People become alcoholics and drink like fish, they become cancer patients and still smoke, they take oxy and go nuts. What the fuck? Some kids huff paint or other household products to get high. Some of us even become nymphomaniacs.

People do all sorts of things to ruin our lives, for whatever reason. Some users become addicts because they want to. Some people get help and “get well” everyday, others don’t.

An addict can break the addictions if they really want to quit. You did.

Most folks who use any of these products responsibly, including ours, never have a problem.”

“Well” Andrew conceded, “In that light you’re right. However I don’t think many citizens will look at the problems in the same way you do.”

Then Andy got back to his original thinking about the huge amount of money Manny was gifting him with.

“Now about the diamonds and the line of credit. It is not in keeping with the Little Man I know. What gives?”

"People change. Is that an answer?” asked the King of Cocaine.

Still a little wary of the strengthening relationship between them, Andrew said “Just among friends Manny, that sounds extremely evasive”

"Just among friends then” Little Man said. “You need to know something about me. A little of which I think you know, some you may have guessed.

There are things you don't know; most of which you would never believe if I didn't tell you.

I think you are aware that I provide the necessities of clean water, electricity, farmland, medical treatment, heat, and anything else if needed, to my compound.

You may have guessed that I also do it for all the villages surrounding us.

I don't think you know or would ever believe, if you didn't hear it from me in person. That I also buy legitimate businesses, which are failing, in my productive areas. I keep thousands of people working; I build schools, roads, hospitals where I know they're needed. I build libraries and arenas in less populated places.

Not many of these projects show black ink at the end of the year, but I make enough in my other endeavors to erase the red ink and fund the adventures that are useful.

Andy, I actually do have an income of billions of U.S. dollars every few months. There is a bundle of net after all expenses.

What am I supposed to do with it? I can't eat it, I can't wear it, I can't live in it, it won't keep me cool in the heat or warm in the cold, I can't fuck it.

I always did hate having anything around me that isn't good for something.

That goes for food, folks, furniture, anything at all. It includes money.

Cash is nothing until you spend it. There is no way in Hell I can spend all I get on me, so I spend as much as I can on things to help my people help themselves.

In spite of all that giving, I am, as you surmised, not the type to do something for nothing.

I do what I do partly for my people and partly for myself. I keep as many of my compatriots as possible satisfied and gainfully employed because of a lesson I learned from one of your country's businessmen.
Specifically from Mr. Ford, who hired as many workers as he could and paid them above the going rate.

When he was asked why he did what he did when he could have kept more profit for himself, Mr. Ford replied that he wanted as many people as possible to be able to buy his cars.

Henry knew his profits would be greater from the large increase in sales to the average person, than if he only sold to the fewer wealthy people.

That strategy worked for Ford then and works for me now. It's a pity that the U.S. has abandoned the Ford Philosophy.

Now is it easier for you to understand my benevolence? Even though it likely shocks the shit out of you, huh?" he asked.

I said, "Let's just say I'm a little bit surprised, but that is still no answer to <u>my</u> question. "Why me?" Part of Little Man's reply was expected. Part of it was not. Not at all.

He said, "There is a new project forming in my mind." Once again Manny said, "You saved my sons' life. Not only did you save Omar's life, you also saved mine.

I was going to storm the capitol to try and rescue Omar. On sober reflection I am sure all my men and I would have been killed.

You, my friend, risked the wrath of a grieving father to bring reason to an unreasonable situation. You convinced me there was a better, safer, way to save my son that was more likely to succeed. You were right. We were successful.

You are the person who can make my project work.

If you will, I want you to bring your talent and intelligence to as many more tortured, abused, misused children as possible. If you will accept a part in this project you will be in absolute control of how to accomplish the objective.
You may do whatever, however, whenever, and wherever it suits you, with full funding from my personal share of the cartel income.

Andrew and Little Man formed a most imperfect union. A drug master and a reformed addict!

A partnership that has been wildly successful.

Honey was given her choice of diamonds from the fourteen-pound velvet bag. She chose a single one-carat marquise cut stone, which she had mounted and worn as a necklace dangling from a gold chain. One stone only.

All the rest of the jewels, she said, were needed for the rescue of the young.

# Chapter 37 Birth of A Beast?

I hope you will forgive me for taking a detour, but I can't shake the nagging question of how it is possible for anyone born in innocence, as we all are, to become the pre-eminent torturing beast that Halle Hernandez became.

I promise to return to business a.s.a.p. However it is imperative for the good of my soul that I go down this road now.

Please bear with me.

Could what happened to President Hernandez have happened to one of us?
Or worse yet could one of our children become so depraved?

After an investigation that I will outline here, I came to know the answer is yes! The evolution to a monster was a consequence that could come to any of us.

Phantom initiated the excursion into the ex-president's life by visiting her birthplace and tracking down all that knew her that were available.

This account will be spotty because some of the people died, others were incarcerated, some moved up in life, still others refused to become involved in my inquiry, and some had simply vanished. The following is the best I could do. It is enough for me to understand her. It may be enough for you also.

Halle lived up to her name for thirty of her forty-two years on this earth.

During the first twelve of those years she and her family lived in squalor.

The child knew, even at such a tender age, that there was more to life than mud and mullion. The girl spent practically every waking minute trying to learn the secret of how other people lived so much better than her family did.

Halle stood at the mouth of the ally her family called home and envied the fortunate kids to the point of tears. Little Senorita Hernandez saw the clean well-fed young girls her age wearing their pretty dresses as they walked along the avenue bordering the place of her dwelling.

A few weeks before her thirteenth birthday was the time that little Miss Hernandez began to live up to her given name.

Halle had been told many times in her young life how beautiful she was and how sexy she would be when she grew up.

Today, so near to becoming a teenager, the Little Miss was feeling very grown-up and wondering if she was indeed beautiful and what did sexy mean?

Perhaps these are the ruminations of every young girl on entering the teens. Perchance some do find the answers they desire.

Not likely the answer fits the dream.

This young girl, Halle would be gifted with answers so eloquent they made her dreams seem to be but petty thoughts, not lifelong ambitions.

Jose, the heavily whiskered, drunken father of one of Halle's small friends came up behind her one day when she stood in the ally. He said, "there is prettiest sexiest little girl I know" and he put his arms around her with both hands on her blossoming breast.

Jose's alcoholic voice whispered in her ear "Muy bonito Chiquita." while his finger rubbed and squeezed her nipples.

Halle was transfixed by surprise at this occurrence. She stood stock-still.
The drunken father of her friend mistook her non-action for consent.

Thinking he was giving the child some adult pleasure he said, "You like when I pinch the tits eh? You sexy little bit. I do more. You like this, then you love if I kiss you tiny pussy.

You want that too, eh?" "I give ten pesos you come along home, Eh?" Halle finally knew what sexy meant. That quick brain she possessed processed the new information in seconds.

That mini minute turned into thirty years of upward mobility, each step of which helped her realize her forename, the significance of which she didn't even know.
She did know her friend's father enjoyed what he was doing and he was willing to pay to do more.

Now Halle wanted to know how badly the drunk wanted to do what he wanted to do.
The little girl was morphing into a woman while still only a dozen years old.

"NO! I don't like what your doing, but you do. How much will you give to touch me like this?" was the answering question.

"What you mean how much?" her friends father said. "I mean what will you give me for letting you put your hands on my tities" she answered.

"Give you?" he laughed, "for this? The drunk said and rubbed her tits, "Nada." and Jose pinched Halle hard. His filthy fingernails dug into her nipples hard enough to cause her pain. "I slap you pretty mouth you say no to me for this," and Jose squeezed again.

"I black you eye you tell what I do. That you get, I get this," and those sharp fingernails dug in again, this time bringing tears to Halle' eyes. "You understand, puta?" said the drunk.

By torturing her breast and saying those hateful words the sot turned an unhappy child into a grown up, world class Bitch.

"You wont do shit," said the street-smart kid "My Dad will kill you if he finds out what you're trying to do to me. Halle said "What do I get if I keep this shit to myself?"

Grumbling to himself Jose stuck his hand in his pocket to bring out the change. He found fifteen pesos. In drunken stupidity he held out his hand and offered the girl five pesos.

Halle snatched the whole hand full of coins and ran.

The drunken pedophile would not have done more damage if he was standing in a pentagram calling forth the Devil.

Jose, Halle's friend's father, later became her first victim.

It is predictable that if a person who would desecrate a child finds an easy babe in the woods, the monster will accost the victim again as soon and as often as it can.

As if there had been no poison in their earlier encounter just two days ago Jose, now shaved and sober, sought out Halle and offered her another thirty-five pesos to come to his house for the kiss between her legs he promised her.

Halle wanted to make him suffer for causing her pain the last time they were together.

Jose, like her own father was a peon. The thirty-five pesos he offered her was a month's income for him. That told Halle how desperate the man was. The mathematician in her said that a kiss on her pussy was worth ten times a squeeze on her tits.

Halle was sure three hundred fifty pesos was more than Jose had, and she was also sure it was much more than he could muster.

Halle decided that letting the bastard know she would let him have what he wanted, and making it his fault he didn't get it, would hurt the idiot more than a slap in the face.

She accepted, but first the price was 350 pesos in advance. Jose left, dejected.

Two weeks later someone knocked on the Hernandez door.
Halle's father took a step back when the opening revealed a Police Force Captain standing there.

"Senor Hernandez?" queried the soldier.
"Si." Miguel Hernandez had long ago learned to fear the police, to always answer their questions, but to volunteer nothing more. "You have daughter, Halle?" was the next query.

"Si." was his reply.

"Buenos. Fetch her." The Captain commanded, "The commandant wants her."

Bewildered, Miguel blurted out "What has she done?" Captain Sabaca looked upon the peon with disdain and with a barely discernable smile on his face the good captain asked, "Are you questioning my authority?"

Miguel hung his head and said "No Captain, never. Please come in, I'll go get the girl now." With that he left to search for Halle and bring her back. When Miguel found his daughter she was with Jose's girl, so he only told Halle he needed her, not mentioning the officer waiting to take her away. As they walked home he did ask his daughter what she had done, where and when she did it, and to whom it was done.

Halle answered every question with "I don't know what you mean Papi. I did not do any thing to anyone."
As soon as Miguel brought his daughter home Captain Sabaca took possession of the girl.

"I'm captain Sabaca. What is your name child?" "My name is Halle, Senor" she replied and then asked, "why do you want to know?"

"The Commander has ordered me to bring Halle Hernandez to him and it was important that I verify your identity."
The Captain said, " It would be a grave mistake, possibly even a deadly mistake, if I brought him the wrong girl."

Upon arrival at the prison, where the Commandant kept his offices, Halle was turned over to a female attendant.

The prison employee looked at her as if Halle was covered in feces.

The child was made to shower and she was dressed in a clean prison uniform before being presented to the Warden.

Armando Chavez, Commander, and Warden, of the local prison said, "Sit down Miss Hernandez."
Halle started to sit in one of the chairs in front of the desk facing him when he said "Sit there." pointing to a large leather chair located beside his ornate desk.

The attendant was dismissed by a nod of Warden's head. Commandant Chavez carefully placed the papers he was perusing on his immaculate desktop. The examination was to be short and to the point.

The Commandant began with an intimidating statement and a personal question "I have heard some interesting things about you Chiquita. Are they true?"

## Chapter 38 Interrogation?

Thirteen-year-old girls who have entered puberty with a bang are difficult to intimidate. The man that she knew frightened his subordinates did not scare Halle. Her experience with the mature opposite sex already implanted in her arsenal another of Life's Great Lessons: Offense is the best defense.

The future president of a large nation did what most good inquisitors do, she responded with a partial answer then replied to the question with a question of her own. "Maybe. What have you heard?" Armando, the man, was intrigued by the girls attitude but Chavez, the warden, was pissed-off by it.

"I ask the questions here. You answer, and only answer. Do you understand or will spending time in a jail cell make you smarter?"

"Yes sir, I understand you." Halle said, adding, "Do you understand me? If you can't tell me what it is you were told and who said it, putting me in a cell will not make me smart enough to answer questions about "something" you heard; Was it that I sometimes bath? I do whenever I can. Was it that I'm poor? I am.
Was it that a man tried to have sex with me? He tried. I didn't let him."

The newly teen-age girl inquired of the Commander. “Is this what you heard?”

Halle then said, “There are hundreds of questions and thousands of answers Commander. Tell me what you heard and I will answer you. I might do more than answer. Maybe I’ll tell you the truth.”

She shut up and waited for him to speak. Again the man Armando, was aroused by her defiance, the Commander side of him was angered by it and determined to teach this rebellious child a lesson. He did teach her a lesson, but his curriculum simply helped build the wall between her and her humanity a few feet higher.

What the commandant said and did next fed the monster, making it larger, stronger, and much more evil.

Chavez: “You bathe when you can? How often is that?

Halle: ”Two, sometimes three times a week.”

Chavez: “Poor? Your father earns nothing?”

Halle: “A little. Doing odd jobs.

Chavez: “You refused sex with a man? Why? Couldn’t he pay your price?”

Halle: “I have no price. I am no puta. I am a virgin. I just didn’t like him.”

Chavez: “Many women do not like their men but they do as they are told. Do you like me?”

Halle: “I do not know you Commander.”

Chavez: “A virgin? Why did he think you would fuck for money? How do you know you wouldn’t like him if you didn’t do it?”

Halle: "I don't know. He said he wanted to kiss my pussy, nothing else. I never tried anything yet and I'm not going to 'til I grow up."
Chavez: "To bad you are not a puta. I would have fucked you and released you, but a virgin? You will be to much fun to let go."
Halle: "What are you talking about? I am not going to be too much fun for you. I am no puta!"
Chavez: "You will do as I tell you, and you will do it willingly."

Halle: "Why do you say that when I just told you I will not."
Chavez: "If you refuse to obey me I will have you locked up with no bath for six months.

I will see to it that your father is never employed so your family will starve, and I will sell you to a madam I know that will beat you into being an obedient whore."
Halle: "You couldn't!"
Chavez: "Oh but I can, and I will.
I am all-powerful here. I do as I wish. I can rape you first and still do all those things.

He went on, "There is another way. You could relax and come to my bed expecting to enjoy sex as you are meant to do."

The Warden said, "Do as I say, and you could bath everyday; your father will be given full-time work. Your family will prosper and in time you will learn to love me."

The Warden ended his threats by saying, "The choice is up to you."

# Chapter 39 Prediction Gone Wrong

You know the choice she made.

Having taken that course, the girl learned fast to be proficient in all of the disgusting acts that Chavez demanded of her.

On her fifteenth birthday Commander Chavez officially announced that Halle was now the Commanders Lady.

This proclamation, changing his whore into his Lady, brought a taste of power to Halle's life. As evidenced by the deference being paid to her by the Commanders troops.

There was one puny, but paramount change in the Wardens predictions at the time of his forced seduction of the girl child.

Halle did not learn to love Armando.
Instead the Commandant fell madly in love with the future President of his nation.

Some of us find acclaim in swinging a bat, or calling a bet, or closing a deal; some of us become famous for painting a picture, or singing a song, or writing a book.

Others of us find our niche in different ways, such as building things that will last for generations, or defacing things meant to last forever; or otherwise desecrating or disassembling things.

Halle found her way to fame when she gained her mastery over the Commander by sucking his cock.

Like most people who use sex for power, not for pleasure, the Commanders Lady did not enjoy the job, but she made Chavez think that to please him was her only goal in life.

Another of Life's Great Lessons:
Tell a big lie, make it big enough, tell it often enough and the stupid will believe it.

The hardening heart of a once innocent child required proof of her power and of her dominance over Chavez. The proof was forthcoming.

Halle demanded the commander send some of his men to exact full revenge for her against an old offender, the first, but far from the last, man to make her want revenge.

She also told Armando precisely what his men were to do to her old friend's father, Jose.

The warden picked three prisoners who were waiting to be executed. He promised to free them if they did precisely as Halle ordered them to do.

The next evening at dusk an enclosed black sedan parked across from the ally where Chavez's Lady once lived, and where Jose, who loved squeezing little girls tits, must pass, on his way home from work.

Jose was tired from his twelve-hour day of hard labor. His head hung down, his back was bent, he longed to get home and lie down.

Jose was not particularly aware of his surroundings, but Halle, in the blacked-out sedan was on high alert.

She grew impatient waiting to learn if the prisoners did as she had ordered them to do.

Two men stepped out of the ally in front of the quarry. One more man came out behind the workman.

Halle was becoming excited as she saw her orders being followed.

The two men in front of Jose stopped, blocking his passage.

The men turned to face him and each of them put a hand on Jose's chest holding him in place.

Jose looked up to see what they wanted as the man behind him pulled his arms backwards.

Halle was getting more and more excited.

She turned up the volume on the parabolic microphone to hear one of the men in front say, "The Commanders Lady wants to know if you like this." Both of the men with their hands on his chest proceeded to twist and squeeze his nipples hard enough to hurt, then hard enough to bring him to his knees. The two men changed their grip from his nipples to his ears with their thumbs placed near his eyes.

Halle was so thrilled she was getting wet between her legs.

The same man who spoke before, apparently the leader of the attackers, now looked down at the man on his knees.

The leader said “The Lady knows you like to kiss a young girls pussy” he was unzipping his trousers as he spoke “Now she wants to know how you feel about kissing a grown mans dick.”

Halle raised a pair of binoculars to better see the tableau unfolding on the street.

The muggers shifted their thumbs to Jose’s eye sockets and increased the pressure until he opened his mouth and accepted a flabby penis.

Halle watched the prisoner’s member becoming stiff as it slipped in and out of Jose’s mouth. She reached her climax before the mugger reached his.

The thrill Halle got watching the leader hold his hand over the mouth and nose of the raped man, forcing Jose to swallow the sperm, was addictive.

Armando’s Lady was anxious for the second part of her commands to commence.

Jose thought that raping him was all they were going to do to him. He was wrong.

Jose was weeping and vomiting profusely when the rest of the Lady’s revenge was enacted.

The actual taking of his manhood was next.

The leader of the trio withdrew. The hoods threw Adrian to the ground on his back.

The second in command took over and pulled the crying mans trousers down to expose his genitals.

The leader then took a pair of shears from his bag and with one snip turned the struggling, sobbing man into a eunuch.

The warden's man threw the still bleeding organ to a nearby cur. The mongrel ate that small part of Jose with gusto.

The first man to ever threaten Halle was the first man she punished so severely. Not the last.

The future leader of the nation sighed with satisfaction. Halle returned to the Commander in high spirits. You might say she was elated by an experience that taught her another one of Life's Great Lessons:

The mighty of the world are those who control the merely powerful.

This little girl who once lived with handouts and hunger was rapidly becoming one of Life's Mighty people.

Halle felt so happy after watching what was done to her long time enemy, that when she went to bed that night she allowed Chavez to do, as he desired.

When the Commander was spent, Halle used her considerable talent in fellatio to restore him to full potency.

The teenaged woman then got on top of him. Straddling his loins she rode Armando as if he was a horse, slapping his face if he didn't buck hard enough.

Armando Chavez was to be her next stepping-stone.

Still groggy the next morning from his all night sexual session, the commandant gave his consent to Halle's request, without really hearing or understanding what she wanted.

She wanted Armando to let her kill the three prisoners that had mutilated Jose.

Halle said she wanted no witnesses to what they had done. No one would be the wiser; the men were scheduled to be executed anyway.

The only difference was that Halle would not just order the deaths but she would also watch the men writhe in agony.

As promised, on order of the Lady to fire, bullets from the firing squad set the three free. Witnessing the execution so stimulated Halle she returned to bed to re-stimulate the worn out Armando.

## Chapter 40 Politico

Every year a member of the Chamber of Senators came to the prison to make an inspection of the facility and to check on its overall operation. This year Halle was introduced to the visiting Senator, and she saw the power of politics.

She paid close attention to the fact that the Commander, who claimed to be all-powerful in the confines of the prison, tended to kiss the Senators ass while the government's representative was visiting.

Halle knew without any doubt that Chavez was number one here in this penal institution.

The new observation of Armando's subservience to Senator Ortez sent the strong message to her that Politicians were more powerful than policemen.

Why she wondered? Why was the commander's power restricted to this bailiwick and why was he the most powerful only when one of the Senators was not present?

The question lingered since the constabulary carried firearms to enforce their demands, while as far as Halle could determine Senator Ortez was defenseless.

Yet, Armando followed him around like a hungry puppy.

Then came a clue as to the commander's sycophantic demeanor.
She overheard Commander Armando Chavez, Commandant and Warden of the nations top-security penitentiary ask if the Senator was going to increase his funding for this assignment.

The lawman was crestfallen when he heard Senator Ortez say, "We are considering where we could best make <u>cuts</u> to the budget not increases."

This evidence of political superiority determined Halle's future.

Logic prevailed, as it always does for the few that use it.

Money outranks Mausers.

Armando and Halle sometimes took Breakfast at a protected table in the main mess hall because they enjoyed the bacon and fried apple dish the prisoners were fed.

Less often they would Lunch in one of the smaller commissaries, however Dinner was never eaten anywhere but alone in the private dining room of their apartment.

Be that as it may, tonight they would share the meal with a guest since Senator Ortez was leaving or the Capital in the morning.

Another step to the realization of the meaning of her name, and the finalization of her transformation into the monster she was becoming, was taken at dinner that evening.

Chavez intended to make the Senators last evening with them memorable so he could make a final play for funding. Halle was ordered to dress as if for a party.

Dinner was a good time. The food was excellent, conversation light, desert delicious.

After the meal the men adjourned to the study to enjoy drinks and Havana cigars.

There were no other females dining to keep Halle Company and the servants would clear the table and clean up. This left the Commanders Lady to fend for herself.

Halle was delighted when, on the way to the other room, Armando told her to get into something more comfortable and join them in the study for a drink before they retired.

Armando Chavez was the first man to fall in love with the beautiful child.

Chavez was the first man to show her how the gentry lived.

The Commander was the first man to allow her some authority, some little amount of power.

The Warden was first to have her sexually, to teach her the variety of fornication.

The leader of the local militia thought he was the first man Halle ever loved.

Armando Chavez, this man of several titles, this seeker of security and of possible advancement, was the first man in Halles life in many ways.

Chapter 41 Hello Papi

Armando Chavez was also the first man to betray her.

When she entered the smoke filled room both men stood.

The Senator indicated a chair near the coffee table for her.
The Warden filled her glass with rum.

She was being treated like royalty and she was quite flattered, especially when she sat down.

That is when she noticed a bulge in the Senator's pants.

Halle was not feeling flattered or excited by the politician's sexual arousal. Rather, she was enthralled by the knowledge that she could possibly control this powerful man through his libido. She was soon to find out.

Armando put down his snifter of brandy and saying his bladder was acting up he left the Senator and Halle alone.

Halle knew instinctively that her patron would not return when she saw the bulge in the politician's trousers grow larger.

Her intuition told the Commanders Lady that that she would soon not be acting Ladylike.

In addition to instinctive knowledge Halle possessed a great deal of ‘street-smarts’. Putting together the facts she was aware of, she knew that The Commandant wanted more money and that The Senator could provide the funding.

Halle further knew the politician was aware that she was living with Armando sans marriage and that the Senator was of the age when men longed for sex with much younger girls, hoping to renew their own youth.

The final brick in the wall of comprehension Halle was building with the mortar of “street smarts” was the penalty for causing Chavez to lose face.

Halle knew what would happen if she did anything to insult, or disappoint the Senator or to otherwise hinder the likelihood of his giving the Warden the funding Armando craved.

The Commandant would surely beat her unmercifully as she had seen him do to prisoners, and even to his own men at times.

Miss Hernandez suspected that they planed for Armando to remain absent so the Senator could make a move on her.

Halle wanted to be wrong. She didn’t love Chavez. Nevertheless the man did provide for her and her family. He did permit her some power, and she was accustomed to the kinds of sexual activity he desired.

The longer Armando was gone, and the closer Ortez moved the conversation toward the personal details of her life, the more convinced the "Commanders Lady" was that she would soon become the "Commanders Coin".

Halle was sure she was being used to convince Ortez to order an increase in the penitentiary's budget. Chavez would, of course, not improve the facility over which he presided.

The increase would simply mean that Armando would have more money to buy more of what he thought of as Luxury and Power.

As usual logic was the victor.

Recognizing this as an opportunity to better her position and perhaps to become the concubine of this evidently more powerful man, Halle submitted gracefully and smiled when the Senator made her kneel between his legs.

When she was able to talk again Halle wiped her mouth and lied to Ortez, saying that the Commander had ordered her to have sex with the Senator. The emerging monster told the Senator that Armando also told her that later on she would have to testify against the Senator in a blackmail scheme Chavez was hatching.

Lowering her eyes, Halle used a bashful, childish voice to inform Cortez that Armando didn't need to order her compliance with the Senator's desire. The developing politician in Miss Hernandez said she had been attracted to the Senator from the moment she was introduced to him.

The “Lady” added, Armando, being much older than she was, should have known how sexually attached she could become to older men.

The aging Senator was convinced the girl really did find him carnally attractive when Halle asked if he would like another demonstration of her fascination for father figures.

The fraudulent femme fatale said she would love to perform for him some more. Anything he wanted.

The Senator said he absolutely would like to enjoy more of her talents, but at another time and in another place.

Halle continued her lies with the words she conjured up while satisfying the aging man. What the young woman said repaid her betrayer ten fold.

Halle told the old man that the Warden was constantly speaking evil of the Chamber of Senators and denigrating its members.

“Including you, sir”, Halle said respectfully. “Armando says you and all the others are a bunch of do-nothing rich slobs that kept cutting wages for the workingman while giving yourselves bigger and bigger raises.”

Arising early in the morning of his departure Senator Ortez joined his host for breakfast and issued an invitation Armando could not refuse.

Ortez invited the Commander and his mistress to an all expenses paid vacation in the Capital City.

The Senator knew Chavez hated opera so, saying he knew the Warden had a lot to take care of before he could leave the prison, Ortez volunteered to take Halle with him so she could enjoy an opera.
At risk of losing his precious raise in salary Chavez literally could not refuse.

The future President left with the Senator. During the ninety-six hours until the Commander joined them, Halle consolidated her case against Chavez, not only with her captive Senator but also with a few other members of the Chamber from whom Ortez wanted to procure favors.

Halle was delighted to act on his wishes; they fit perfectly with her own recent political ambitions. The brand-new vote seeker promised to do anything for her new protectors friends they wanted her to do. Halle was surprise by how few of them wanted her on her back. It was a testament to the girl-woman's skill that each of the men was made to believe that he was her favorite.

The Commandant wore a great smile on his face as he stepped from the limousine the Senator sent for him.

Armando felt much more important when he saw there were two columns of six armed guards in dress uniforms standing at attention beside the automobile. Armando Chavez thought lending Halle to the Senator was a great idea. He thought it made him a terrific ally who had sent an Honor Guard to welcome him to the Capital.

## Chapter 42 Welcome to The Capitol?

I certainly hope there never comes a time in your life that you are as wrong about anything as this vanity-ridden dolt was about the Honor Guard.

The half dozen guards were in dress uniforms to avoid unwanted publicity.

Armed soldiers in their finest were nothing if not common in the seat of government, whereas death squads were rarely seen in public and earned a great deal of public exposure if they were.

Chavez left the car, and the smile left his face, and for all practical purposes Armando, left the planet.

The smile vanished, and was replaced by sheer panic as the guards took the traditional arrest formation on each side of a prisoner.

Another official sedan appeared at the end of the street and Senator Cortez got out. Halle followed close on the Senator's heels and took the politicians arm.

The panic turned to hope when Armando saw his Lady, and a grin started to decorate his mouth again after Halle motioned for him to join her and Ramundo.

Relief washed over him as the Commander rushed to embrace his friends.

Armando made it five paces toward the couple before the guards shot and killed him.

As Cortez ordered the armed escort to do to do if the disgraced Commander made any threatening gesture aimed at the Senator or Miss Hernandez.

The last image on the dying mans retina was that of his smiling, no, not smiling, of his smirking underage ex-concubine.

Halle rose in the political ranks as she did everything else, mostly on her back and knees. The monster she had become fucked, sucked, blackmailed, killed and on rare occasion even voted her way to the top job.

The unfortunate partners in her peccadilloes, all paid a price for their allegiance to the rising politician.

Once in office President Hernandez made sure the people loved her by simply listening to them, and responding to their needs.

Whenever the people's needs did not conflict with her own desires.

Halle soon turned the democracy into a kind of monarchy.

Halle could be President for life by popular acclaim. No one knew how she really ruled, except anyone foolish enough to oppose her.

# Chapter 43 Devils Not

I felt sorry for the evil transformation into what the innocent young girl Halle became.

At the same time I knew that the monster President Hernandez deserved to end as she did. Cold, hungry, alone, and used for anything, by anyone that felt the need.

Now we will return to the mission Honey and Andrew were on.

Andrew opened the first Devils & Angels and began to take kids, teens, and young adults off the streets.

The rescued children were moved from one club to another 'till it was no longer possible for their tormentors to trace them. These kids were fed, dressed, housed, employed, educated, and given back their sense of self-worth.

More often than not, the source of their abuse was severely punished.

Honey ended her narrative with "That's it. The whole ball of wax. The Alpha and Omega. The complete enchilada. However the hell you want to say it.
At least it was 'till Andy suddenly disappeared."

Scruffy raised his head from Honey's lap where he pretended to be napping, and looking first to Honey then to me, he barked three short barks.

As if she understood dog language Honey said "Oh yeah, Scruffy reminded me you're a private dick. Prove your worth and Find Andrew Smyth. What is your fee anyway? Never mind. Find Andy safe and sound and I'll give you whatever."

"Deal" I said. Joking, I added, "If Scruffy agrees." And I'll be damned, the dog barked. Twice. Then he laid his head back down and I guess he really did go to sleep.

The picture of a sad looking canine, a mule named Honey, an international drug dealer, and a missing Mafioso.

You tell me one good reason a combination like that would keep me from the delicious home cooked meals, stimulating conversations, loving arms, and other comforts of home just to find a missing crook turned do-gooder?
As hard as I tried I can't think of any. Not one single reason; Naturally I called home and told Nora not to expect me 'till she saw me.

In my mind the only thing sweeter than sugar is the satisfaction of a job well done.
Or of a job medium rare if there is a little blood involved.
As is customary, I'll start this investigation from the back and intensely work toward the front.

What am I looking for:
A man tightly connected to the world's largest drug cartel.

A man responsible for the abduction and the probable murder of a nations leader.
A man being personally funded by Little Man, one of the worlds deadliest, most vengeful, most dangerous of humans.
A man recently a boss in the Family.
A man once a drug dealer.
A man once a drug addict himself.
A man now fairly well regarded by respected citizens but mostly trashed by the trashier denizens.
A man now a person hell-bent on rescuing young people.
A man now missing.
Putting last things first, the question is why is Mr. Smyth gone?

Jumping to, or as is my wont, hurtling to, a conclusion. I surmise that he could have chosen the wrong body to pick up off the streets.

A supposition that begs the question, was it the body itself, or is it someone holding the other end of a leash attached to Andrews's choice that is upset with him?

Picking people is a lot like harvesting apples. You must go to the tree that produces them. With this fruit it is not an apple tree, it is the inner city, the slums, the city jails, the failed schools.

Some of these apples do fall far from their roots. You look for the bad ground the good body fell on, then try your best to keep her or him from rotting.

Andy must have spent a lot of time gathering the information needed to make the appropriate selections to rescue.

I spoke with fifteen of the soberest inhabitants of the seamier side of the city I was in. I asked each one of them if they had any knowledge of a man offering to help them find a job and a place to live.

Twelve of the least polite of the fifteen told me to fuck off. Two said to shove it up my ass.

Number fifteen said a guy made him that offer last month, but the man never came back. When number fifteen told Gus, his pimp, about the offer the pimp told him to forget it nothing would happen. Gus knew the ass-hole wouldn't be back.

This statement punched my curiosity button. How did the pimp know the man was not coming back? I asked the boy when his pimp told him that nothing was going to happen.

The young man said it was the same night the offer was made, soon after he told his pimp about the encounter. The kid also said he should have known the guy couldn't do nothing when the prick said his name was Smith.

How phony can you be he wondered, using a name like Smith.

When I offered to take him wherever he wanted to go number fifteen said no.

## Chapter 44 15 Again

The boy told me Gus said that if he tried to leave, the pimp would find him and kill him.

I put my offer on the shelf, and since it was getting late I put myself to bed. I wanted to be fresh the next day.

I awoke around noon, got dressed and fed, called Nora and I went to work.

I hailed a cab. In fact I called several cabs until I found the right one, one driven by a cabbie that knew about Gus and could take me to his digs.

Gus Cochran lived in a brownstone on the edge of the more affluent section of the city.
I knew nothing about him other than that he was a pimp; therefore he was a part of the scum of the world.

Pimps are slaveholders pure and simple. These flesh-peddlers force the whores to perform and they punished those that didn't.

I am a great fan of consensual sex.
All kinds of sex in all positions and in any variation. The operating and indispensable word though is "consensual."

If it is some pimps unwilling bitch, a broad you just met, a long time girl friend, or even your wife, if you're burning your wick in an unwilling candle that makes you nothing but a low-life rapist. Without agreement between the participants any form of sex is undisputed rape.

Of all the kinds of crime there are, I consider forcing involuntary prostitution, rape, to rank in the worst three types of all time.

In case you were wondering, It is my opinion murder and abduction are the other two.

You can now imagine the mood I was in when I knocked on the door of the son-of-a-bitch that pimped out Denny, the sixteen year old kid that was #15.

If your brain is still busy wondering if you have ever taken a no to actually mean yes and inadvertently raped anyone, I'll describe what I was feeling.

Cochran opened the door and his fucking lights went out! I cold-cocked the bastard before the squeak in the hinge had ended.

I dragged the unconscious man into the house and shut the door.

A giggle came from the other room when I slapped Gus hard on the face to wake him up. Turning toward the sound I saw a boy standing in a doorway apparently unaware that he was naked from the waist down.

The young man appeared to be thirteen or fourteen years old. The long red marks, a few of them turning into dark bruises on his legs, indicated that he was recently beaten with a whip.

Regardless of his condition the kid had a smile a mile wide plastered to his mug. He split his ear-to-ear grin by saying "Hit him again for me."

I said, "Get dressed and get your shit together. We're leaving here in a few minutes," then I honored the 'teens request.

Gus woke up feeling the pain in his face. "Who the fuck are you and what do you want?" were his first words to me.

Another of Life's Great Lessons is that you catch big fish with big chunks of the bait that you know they like.

I became a delicious big chunk of chum when I said, "Andrew Smyth is my partner.

You met Andy when he offered to take one of the children you've been miss-using off the street."

The boy came in the room carrying a paper bag. "This is all I've got," he said.

"That's okay" I told him, "I'm gonna get you some clothes, a place to sleep and a job as soon I have a little chat with your friend here." I spoke so the pimp could hear me make the same promise to the waif that Andy was making to the kids.

Turning to Gus I said "You know the drill dip-shit we can do this the easy way for me or the hard way for you but we are going to do this.

I want to know what you did with Mr. Smyth and I want to know where he is now."

"O.K. Mack, take it easy." Wheedled the scum through a mouth bleeding from my blows, "I didn't do nothin' with the guy and I got no idea where he is now.

## Chapter 45 The Ending

All I done was tell Julie what the fucker told my nephew."

I shuddered to think of this, or any, kid being related to Gus. "The boy you horse-whipped is really kin to you?" I queried. "Hell no man" came the answer "all those little cock suckers are good for is to bring me money. I call 'em all nephew 'till they're used up and I get rid of 'em."

"Exactly how do you do that? Get rid of them I mean?" He said. "Like we all do, I sell 'em to Julie."

"You keep saying that name but you don't tell me who or where this Julie is.

Cough it up, give me some details on Julie." I said.

"Why not?" the pimp shrugged, you're new in town. Everybody knows Julie is the wop that pays cash for old whores.

Nobody knows what he does with them but they go away in a day or two.

They say Julie can make anyone go away for cold cash so you better be careful who you smash in the mouth." Gus said with malevolence streaming from his eyes.

"Thanks for the warning Cochran," I said, "I'll be sure to watch my step" as I brought my foot down hard on his shin.

The punk howled in pain.

I said "I'm tired of this game now you shithead. Where the hell is Andrew Smyth?"
"I don't know I tell you, I don't fuckin' know!" he wailed.

As he saw my fist cock back to slam him again Cochran shouted, "Stop, please! The last I heard he was at the Depot, Julies bar on Fife Street, that's all I know. "Don't hit me again, I can't tell you anything else." Cochran begged, "Honest to God I don't know anything else."

"Honest to God?" I said, "I don't think you can be honest even with God. I do know if you're lying to me now you will soon be face-to-face with that Supreme Being.

The Depot was indeed a depository, the contents of which I would be reluctant to associate with either on a business or social level.
Are you familiar with the phrase "the dregs of society?"
If not, spend a few minutes in the Depot and you'll get acquainted rather rapidly.

Toothless faces, disease ridden bodies, mentally incompetent souls, all bellied up to an unclean bar.

Wasted humanity in a decrepit setting. What could be more depressing?
If you have the answer keep it to yourself. This is bad enough for me.

A couple of ceiling fans slowly turned, attempting to circulate a breeze.

The fan only succeeded in distributing a disgusting odor throughout the unkempt room.

Cochran swore he thought this was the last place Andy might have been.
I mentally held my nose and walked further into the squalor.

Scarcely visible in the dim light was a metal door on the far wall.
Moving carefully across the room I knocked on the door then pounded on it when there was no response.

No interest was shown in me at all until I finally kicked the entrance in hard and loud.

Life got a lot more interesting in a hurry after I made enough noise.

That final flurry of franticly forcing the forbidding fissure in the flat face of the wall to falter, brought a furious fat fellow out of the foyer of the fabulously furnished, furtive flat found behind the door separating the fine room from the filthy bar.
In other words I kicked the damned door in and a big brute came barreling through the opening straight at me.
I easily disposed of the repulsive critter by using his own momentum to send him smashing into some nearby tables.

# Chapter 46 Julie

I wish the door had been painted green. Then I could use an infamous porno title for the next chapter.

Behind the Green Door, now a totally destroyed portal, away from the shitty bar, was a very nicely appointed office.

So? I was too weak to resist using the porn title. Besides I liked the damned flick. So what? Didn't you ever do anything stupid?

Getting back to my search for Andrew Smyth. After launching the blimp of a bodyguard into the den of the dying I entered the office expecting to find the infamous Julie I had heard so much about.

What I did discover in the package behind the splintered doorframe was another surprise.

I found an unperturbed, coiffed and costumed dapper dude sitting behind an ornate gilded desk.

"May I offer you something?" he said with a quizzical smile on his lips.

"Are you Julie?" I asked.

"The way you announced your arrival, without invitation I might add, one would think you knew on whom you were calling.

In light of your conspicuous ignorance I'll chose to impart your requested information. Yes, I am Julie."

"Then you may indeed offer me something." I answered his earlier query. "Produce Andrew Smyth alive and well."

"Would that I could. Mr?" he said. "Phantom" I supplied to his unfinished question.

"Phantom?" he mused "An odd nom d' plume I think. Is it fitting? Do you move without detection? Are you an hallucination? Insubstantial? An apparition?" the fop asked.

Julie continued speaking in his contemplative mood,

" I certainly hope so, for none of them can be more than a nuisance to me."

"Nightmare" I said "A definition you chose to omit. Your worst nightmare as most people like to amend it.

In your situation the amendment is beyond factual, it is visceral. In fact, If you cannot grant my request or don't provide me with the information to retrieve my partner, you will no longer be of use to me."

"If I am no use to you, then you may leave," replied the sissy man.

"It's not hard to see that you are of no use to anyone else, so if you can't help me then perhaps I should rid the world of you."

All of this was spoken in a very camaraderie voice. The next statement was made in flat, deadly threatening tones, "One piece at a time."

The grinning tinker bell pushed a bell, located under the edge of his desk, summoning four body builders. They entered through a concealed door in the back wall.

"Speaking of pieces," Julie said with a hint of humor "I'll just let these bad boys pick yours up when they get exhausted by tearing you to bits."

The four strong men protecting Julie were so effective in the past that Julie didn't even stand up. He wanted to watch my devastation in the comfort of his throne-like chair.

Thank goodness I try to keep my bases covered. It did occur to me that someday I could be faced with more than just a street brawl so I studied martial arts defense systems.
Because I wasn't able to do so for so many years, now I go for the best of whatever it is I need.

Since I am capable of it, I mastered Krav Maga; an art that I am told was designed for the Israeli Defense Forces. Krav Maga practitioners are not trained just to defend themselves, but also to kill the opponents.
The four bullyboys hired to defend Julie were also paid to entertain him as they did their job with demonstrations of death.

When the melee started, one of the goons said, "I am a black belt master and you will soon be a smashed piece of shit."
I saved him for last.

# Chapter 47 Turntable

By the time number three went down you could see the sweat on that one's face and the fear in his eyes. The fear must have infected his brain because the hotshot idiot tried a frontal attack on me. Too bad the braggart didn't know Krav Maga.

Standing amid the four bodies of men who no doubt richly deserved the end they came to, I turned my attention once again to Julie. I can only imagine that Julie, watching me decimate his bullyboys, must have felt like Nero did while watching Rome burn.

To my definite consternation the small man showed no sign of concern in his demeanor. In fact the slight figure struck me as if he thought he was still in control of the game.

Turns out, he was.

Julie said in his most sanctimonious voice "Mr. Phantom you had best hope that your name is a factual representation of who you really are and not merely poetic."

"My name is apt," I said. I then went on to say "and does the name Julie mean insufferable fairy? If that is a true interpretation then your name too is appropriate."

"An awkward retort." The fop replied, "You may not make the attempt to be so glib if I furnish the enlightenment for which you are searching. Nevertheless I have decided to grant your wish."

"I'll bet these four," I said with a sweeping gesture of my hand "wish you had made that decision six minutes ago."

"Be that as it may, I changed my mind about killing you when it occurred to me that the Family might like to have a word or two with you"

That little speech did two things.
First, it ushered in a trio of dangerous looking men, made even more dangerous by the drawn guns they held. Each pistol pointed unwaveringly at me.

I could have been the inventor of Krav Maga and faster than Usain Bolt, but it didn't take a genius to know I can't outrun, or out fight, a bullet.

I stood perfectly still and raised my hands in surrender.

The trio exercised very good judgment by handcuffing my legs as well as my hands after they saw for themselves what I did to their four cohorts before them.

Julie, it appears, has won this round, in as much as I threw in the towel. The unfunny little fellow should bear in mind though that most bouts are fought for <u>twelve</u> rounds, unless one of the opponents in the ring is K.O.d. early.

If you run into Julie, tell the little wart to be warned, I am still standing. Don't count me out.

Notwithstanding my dire thoughts, I am trussed up like a Christmas turkey, in chains and getting delivered to gang headquarters because a person who fancy's old whores thinks some criminals might like a word with me.

Julie, the diminutive dude from the Depot was right again. Someone in the Family did want words with me. Not just someone, it was Peter Paulson, the current head of the Family. Everyone in the organization called him 'Papa.'

I wanted to have several words with him.

Paulson looked to be in his late forties or early fifties. This forced interview was the first time I saw Papa Paulson and he was another unpredictable sight.

He looked like a man you wanted as your best friend.

The head of a criminal enterprise, in my eyes at least, should not look like a choirboy.
This man routinely ordered violent acts, even murders, to be carried out by his subordinates.

Yet he looked so damned innocent.

Here comes another of Life's Great Lessons: Never judge a book by its' cover!

The pages of Paulson's life would not read like a mystery. On the contrary his life is quite transparent. Just check his rap sheet.

Papa was a pre-teen thief and gang member, a teenage rapist and an enforcer.

In his early twenties Paulson was a gang leader, recruiter, and killer.

His late twenties found Peter to be second in command of two large gangs. Simultaneously! Impossible?

Not for someone as devious and insidious as Peter (Papa) Paulson.

In his late thirties Papa consolidated the four most powerful gangs in the state to form the Family.

Anyone who can do what he did when and how he did it is not stupid. He was cruel yes, but stupid? Never.

When I was brought before the boss of the Family, Paulson proved his prudence with his first question, which was, "How can we in the Family be of service to satisfy your need?"

Papa was direct and polite, but I was still in shackles. I said, "You can take these irons off to begin with." "Very well" he agreed, motioning to one of his minions. "Get our guest a chair and make him as comfortable as possible."

.

## Chapter 48 Another First

An overstuffed armchair was produced, my cuffs were removed and I was invited to sit.

"We shouldn't continue this conversation as strangers" the gang boss said, "My name is Pete Paulson, and you are?"
"Charles Phantom" I answered.

"Mr. Phantom I feel it is my duty to let you know that my friends are well aware of how dangerous and destructive you can be. For that reason if you make any move that even hints at your leaving the chair you're sitting in, you will be killed."

"Thank you for being so straightforward with me." I replied, "but I knew the stooges in the corners behind you with their hands in their jacket pockets are holding pieces trained on me.

Call me Charley, Pete. We might as well be less formal now that we are issuing warnings to each other."

"And what is your warning for me Charley?" asked Papa.
"I would rather call it a heads–up." I answered.
I was beginning to play a high-stakes game of mental poker with Papa.

"You must know that I am not alone in this. I am not as strong as you, but a friend of mine is much more powerful than you are."

I continued my bluff saying, "My friend knows precisely what I'm doing and where it's being done. If I come to harm, for any reason, my friend will exact a high toll.

A re-payment high enough to eliminate the Family wherever it exists and to bring you face to face with him.

My friend will want you alive if possible, but in zip-lock bags if need be."

I went on with a smile on my face "Now let us see how we can be of service to satisfy each others needs, O.K.?"

Papa wore no smile, but he wasn't frowning either when he asked, "Who is this mega man?"

I said, "Where is Andrew Smyth?"

"So?" said Paulson "This is all about one of my lieutenants. I assume you do know that Mr. Smyth is a trusted member of the Family?"

"I do know a lot about Andy, but I don't know his current location. You do. It will benefit both of us for you to tell me where he is." I said.

"Will a little thing like that call off your dogs Charley?" he wanted to know.

"That would be a beginning." I replied.

"And the ending?" He asked.

Andy's safe return to our fold will write finish to the abduction of one of your "trusted Lieutenants." I said.

"How will you and your all powerful friend feel if Mr. Smyth refuses your courageous rescue?" Papa asked.

"A trusted member of the family needs rescued from you?" I said with feigned surprise "I thought he just needed the opportunity to make his own decisions."

"The interpretation of words doesn't change the answers. If he refuses?" said Peter with some slight annoyance.

I answered honestly "That all depends on if and why he refuses."

Then I embellished my answer by adding a supposition "On the other hand, if Andy wants to rejoin me, and you allow him to do so unhindered, my very powerful friend will take your kindness as a personal favor."

Then I played the card to win the hand. "My friend may help your businesses grow, including voluntary prostitution, or any of your other avocations."

"Why should I think your un-identified companion can work these miracles?" said the skeptical Papa.

Honey did say Little Man told Andrew if he ever needed anything to call on him. Andy needed something now. Mentally I dropped the dime on

Papa for Smyth. I called on Manny In a surreptitious way, of course.

Acting as if I had Mr. Smyth's Power Of Attorney, I took a deep breath and a shaky chance, and then said with as much confidence as I could muster "All I will say is my buddy is a little man living in the south."

Without any question Papa got my message. As incredible as it might be, Papa Pete Paulson, head honcho of one of the nations largest and most dangerous crime syndicates, blanched.

Paulson turned nearly as pale as toilet paper.

Within minutes an unshaven, disheveled, confused looking Devil of Devils & Angels was brought before us.

I was theoretically his partner but he and I had never met, so as soon as he walked in I greeted him with "Damn Andy it sure is good to see you again.

Honey sends her love and is anxious for you to come home so we can keep on in our latest campaign to save the abused. I really am glad to see you" I repeated, "We were worried that some idiot had killed you or something."

Andy didn't look on top of his game, but he caught on immediately. "It's good to see you too partner but what are you doing here? He said, "You have nothing to do with my problem."

"Let's get out of here, I'll fill you in back at the office." I said, "Honey is waiting for us."

Having no desire to join the Family or any other reason to prolong my stay among thieves, I decided to press my luck.
Putting my arm around Andy I guided him to the exit saying to Paulson "I'll make sure my friend knows that we owe you one Papa."

"Good Charley, for that I'll owe you too."
We walked away with no one attempting to dissuade us.
We went back to the Angel of Devil & Angel

Honey laughed, and cried, and hugged, and hit, and finally sat down and started asking Andy questions.
Was he O.K.? Did they hurt him? What the hell did he do to make the Family mad enough to pick him up?

Andrew answered her.
Yes. No. Nothing. It was not what he did; it was what they thought he had.

Andy said, "I took half a million in cash down south and didn't bring it back."
"Papa thinks I stashed the cash for a later recovery."

Honey broke in with "Halle Hernandez took that money when she arrested us."

"I told him that." Andrew replied, "Papa didn't believe me and I have no proof that she did take it. I honestly have no idea where the money is."

I explained how I set Smyth free.

The three of us celebrated our success, and I left to give the lovers time to express their happiness in a more personal way.

Scruffy came with me.

Honey came with Andy.

The morning came with opportunity.

I had just showered, shaved, and dressed when a soft knock on my door accompanied Honeys dulcet tones asking if I was up and decent.

I tapped on the nightstand while saying that I was still sound asleep and that my wife thinks I am more than decent, she thinks I'm terrific.

# Chapter 49 Tail Waggen' Time

Honey said, "It's a shame that you're still sleeping because breakfast is being served.

I think it's great that your wife thinks you're already terrific," Miss Potter continued, "So I can tear up this check you were going to get for fifty grand?"

"Damn, all that pounding on my door woke me up" I yawned, "what's on the table?"

Still only half awake, I stumbled into the kitchen to be greeted by another surprise.

My life seems to be full of the serendipities of existence since I became friends with Scruffy.

There was more than eggs benedict at my place setting

The knife was resting on the aforementioned check for fifty-K, the fork was placed, tines down, on a blank check, and the bowl of the spoon was filled with tiny question marks.

What a way to break a fast. A puzzle within a puzzle within an enigma.

"Looking at my repast I take it that I awoke to a challenge." I said, "I'll start with the question marks. With no other clue I will take the easiest answer, which is, you have many doubts about me.

Next the fork is positioned as if I was going to take a bite of the check.
Since there is no figure on the paper I am being offered a blank check.

That means I could command any amount for whatever it is that you might seek.

As we all know the knife suggests a cut, it is resting on the check you offered me for services performed.

The first thing to occur to me is that you want to know if I'll take a cut, something less than you offered.

First guesses are often wrong; so I thought of another, more fitting answer.
Now that my ducks are in a row the answers should be easy.

If you are not questioning me, then you are asking what I want. I want to go home. I miss my wife and son.

The knife is probably asking if I want to cut in on your action. No I don't, I am not actually sure of what your action is.

That check will remain blank. No amount of money can keep me from spending a few weeks with my family between jobs.

As far as the knife is concerned I did not stipulate a fee for the service I performed.

We agreed that you would pay only what you thought my result was worth. I will accept as payment in full whatever you think is adequate.

I admit that Andrew came home within a short time after I started my investigation but the job was not as easy as it might have looked.

There were a few complications; nevertheless it was not the most difficult thing I've ever done. In view of those facts you may change your opinion of how much it was worth to you for me to bring Andrew home, unscathed, from Papa's Family. The figure may be adjusted from anything to nothing."

"Just in case you're asking if I want to be paid to keep quiet about your action," I went on, "that answer is no, not on your life."

There was an immediate objection. Speaking in unison they said, "No, no, that's not it." Andy went on to say "We would never believe you to be capable of extortion.

"I know there is at least one more interpretation," I said, "It could also mean that you want to know how much it would take for me to do more jobs for a piece of the pie my last check was cut from."

"That's a lot closer to the true solution" Honey said "the fifty thousand was not nearly what it was worth to me to get Andy back safe and sound. It just seemed like a nice round figure. There is more where that came from if that was not enough."

"No Honey" I replied, " that's more than enough, but thanks for the offer."

Andrew broke his silence by interjecting "Mark you are within striking distance of the meaning of our puzzle.

After what I saw you do with the family and the things Honey told me about you, I knew you would be as close as anyone could come to putting the correct pieces together.

The puzzle was just to make sure you were wide-awake. Most of the display was as you said it was. The blank check does mean you can name your own fee. The knife does mean you may cut your piece of a very large pie.

The only error was the spoon full of questions. It is not a matter of what do <u>you</u> want. Rather, it is a question of what <u>we</u> want."

Unsure of the destination of this line of conversation, I decided to make a few observations. "Just what is it you want?" I asked. Before the answer came I said, "Here are a few things you should know.

I do not engage in the drug traffic. I am not a racketeer. To be straight with you, I prefer catching criminals to being one; even if my specialty is burglary when I'm not busy, as a private eye.

I have absolutely no knowledge of the drinking and dining business. As a consequence I would be of no value to running the Devils & Angels.

I <u>will</u> be glad to accept you as clients of Phantom Investigations for legitimate cases.

## Chapter 50 An Offer I Can't Refuse

Other than for legal inquiries I don't see how I can be of service to you."

Andy and Honey broke into huge smiles. Honey said, " Do I look like a mule to you? No long ears, no little tail flicking flies off of the tail I sit on."

Andrew chimed in with "We are not racketeers. We no longer deal in drugs.
I'll bet you are a damned good second story man, but we are strictly legitimate, so we can't use a burglar.
Honey runs Devils & Angels better than either one of us could.

That leaves catching criminals or being one. If you choose catching over being then we want you with us. You can take us on as exclusive full time clients if you want to. I don't give a damn how you come in.

We need a man of your gifts and talents to join us in what is turning into a never ending quest."

Andy's eyes reflected an honest plea as he said, "We, Honey, Little Man, and I, want to know if you would care to team up with us in our effort to help some of the hapless kids working the streets."

"Never ending quest? You got that right!" I said, "Pay-for-play sex has been around for centuries. It's legal in most of the world.

In olden times it was considered an honor to have a daughter offer her body for pleasure in the temples of the Gods. In the ancient Greek world selling sex was more or less a religious act. You can check on it in any neighborhood library.

Isn't it amazing how things have changed? In the puritanical U.S.A. today most sexual contact is considered immoral, and some acts are illegal even between married couples.

From revere to revile in a few short centuries, Crazy is it not?

I wonder how many of todays raving beauties realize that every time they put on lipstick, especially, the bright red variety, they are wearing a product invented by the ancient temple prostitutes of Greece? Those young ladies colored their lips to advertise that they were available for oral sex.

The message was never officially changed, and the products remains the same, except there are more colors to chose from.

So are housewives and call girls both unknowingly, or perhaps they're fully aware, still saying to the world that they will "go down" on their partners?"

Smyth said, "I know that attempting to erase the world's oldest business is not only never ending, it is an impossible task."

Honey said, "We're not suggesting that we end the profession. I'm talking about saving the children that are <u>forced</u> into prostitution every day."

Andy said, “You would think that performing that service for one city would be possible, but I am beginning to think not; At least not without a lot of help. Every time we pick four off of the street it seems like eight more show up.”

“You don’t know why?” I asked with a hint of disbelief in my voice. Hearing no reply I continued, with the solution. “You are concentrating on removing the kids from the traffic.
You can’t think these underage whores thought this up all by themselves can you?

If they did go into this line of work on purpose how long do you think they could remain on the street as independent operators before they were ‘recruited’ by the pimp that claimed the territory the kid was working? One night? Two?

If your mission wasn’t cemented into the experience of saving Little Mans boy and tied up with the Drug lords purse stings, maybe logic could live in your thought process.”

Honey broke into my narrative angrily, “Hey cowboy loosen the lasso. Andy risked his life for that kid.”

Smyth said, in a calmer way, “It’s alright Honey, Mark is voicing a valid opinion. This is Guzmahn’s idea. Manny <u>is</u> bankrolling the operation because we saved Omar.
The part Mark may have missed is that Guzmahn is not using cartel money but he is paying out of his own pocket.”

"Also the "Drug Lord" gave free rein on when, how and where we use the funds.
Little Man's only request is that we try to save as many kids as we can.

From your remarks I am positive there is a better way than the path we are on.
I would really appreciate hearing your solution to our problem."

I could not accept as fact that people as intelligent as Andy and Honey strike me as being, would not have arrived at, or hell might even have been born with, the answer to such a simple problem.

I started with a reiteration of what I consider universal knowledge.

"There is no one way to do what you are trying to accomplish. You can't cure anything by correcting symptoms, you must remove the source of the problem." Then I continued with specifics.

"The only way to stop the influx of child prostitutes is to stop the pedophiles from kidnapping the kids and turning them into whores, to correct the family conditions that encourage children to run away, and to stop the pimps that find the runaways on the streets and take control of the kids."

"You have just demonstrated the reason we need you." Andrew said. "You are un-encumbered by my friendship with Manny or the history of our mission. Logic rules your interpretation of information."

That same logic must tell you that it is not possible to do what you say must be done to fulfill our goal. Now what?"

My answer is short and sweet. Well short anyway. "Your assignment was to save as many kids as you can, not to save every damned kid in existence. That is possible to do."

Honey's retort was also short but definitely not sweet "Why in hell do you think we would ask some know-it-all like you to partner up if we didn't believe you would be an asset instead of an ass?"

"Now, now, Honey don't be vitriolic," said Andy, "We all have our weaknesses." Then Smyth looked at me and said, "Mark we both believe you could be a great boon to our effort.
Will you join us and bring your huge imagination and indisputable sense of logic to our aid?"

With a little tongue-in-cheek, I gave him the same answer I was going to give the first time he asked, "Certainly I'll help, if only to prove to Honey that flattery works better than sarcasm, and under the conditions that I've stated. Deal"?

"Deal!" Once again they spoke in unison and I became a member of the Devils And Angels subsidiary.

Taking my own advice I spent some three weeks at home with my wife and son.
I was on vacation and I insisted that Nora and Matt also go on vacation with me.

# Chapter 51 Vacation Time

The last time the three of us took time-off together it turned into a working vacation, so I had to promise them that this time it would be just the family. <u>Our</u> family not <u>The</u> Family.

We went to Nome Alaska. It was far more beautiful and a lot warmer than the travel brochures described the city to be.
We thoroughly enjoyed the two weeks living with Emperors.
This royalty strutted in the snow banks with other penguins and it was our pleasure to strut at their side.

No, I did not write by the light of Rudolph's' red nose.

On the twenty-first day of our Artic adventure it was time to go back to the States.
As usual, Nora was teary eyed in my embrace as we kissed so-long.

Matthew, once again, wanted to attend my absence and assist in one of my investigations.

I wanted to give it up and stay home with my family.

The slings and arrows of outrageous fortune beset me, as they always did, and I was far to lacking of virtue to do nothing. I left.

Part of my heart knows remaining out of the action, by retiring to the comforts and pleasures of home would likely be terrific.
Another part of the pump would always grieve for those in need; as would the organizations I support that help people in the position I once was in.

Now I am in a position to donate to good causes, to contribute to the world by helping many people in need of aid.
If I left the field of battle my income would probably not allow me to fight the good fight with them.

I would be surrendering my weapons for purely selfish reasons. That fact alone would stain the fabric of my retirement.

Another of life's great lessons: Those to whom much is given, much is expected.
There is no doubt the lesson applies to me.

Twenty-two days after leaving the meeting with Honey and Andrew my plane touched down on the Devils and Angels private tarmac.

Thirty minutes later I sat facing Mr. Smyth and Miss Potter over a beautiful oak pedestal table while we enjoyed several cups of real Columbian coffee. We discussed the unfeasibility of accomplishing all of the necessary steps to eliminate the abuse of children and young adults.

We agreed that kidnappers should be left to law enforcement.

We agreed that convincing children not to run away from home was the job of the parents.

We also came to the decision that educating families are the domain of State Job and Family Services.
There was only one avenue left for us to explore. That street led directly to the flesh-peddlers.

Having had some prior experience in that area, in the person of Gus Cochran, I suggested the pimp path was the one for me to walk.
Andrew and Honey would sustain their current efforts, which were effective in freeing some of the pimp prisoners.

After accepting the assignment of turf the three of us ate a breakfast of steak, eggs, and grits while discussing where to begin the new assault on childhood prostitution.

I didn't need a starting point. I already had one; it was a visit to Papa Paulson.
There is only one reason Papa would take a seat with anyone. That ticket to talk to Papa was stamped "profit."

In order to see Papa Paulson again it was necessary to go back and have another session with the man whose business was rooted in the acquisition of dead souls. I had to enter the world of the lowest form of humanity. I returned to the Depot.

Julies gushed, "Well, Mr. Phantom you are the slippery one. I never dreamed you would grace my door again."

That greeting revealed more than the fairy wanted me to hear. He sounded more surprised than he should have been.
Julie didn't expect to see me again because he thought I was dead.
My appearance, after my supposed death suggested Julius was out of favor with the Family.

That misinformation could only have come to the sissy through Mr. Paulson.
The revelation was that Julie was of so little value to the Family that Papa lied to him.

I was sure that the little man that trafficked in used whores for some unknown reason must have counted on Papa for something.

"How would you like to get even tighter with Papa?" I queried. He did as was expected and answered my question with a question.
"How can I or anyone, for that matter, be tighter with the Family than I am right now?"

"Tell Papa you can make him more money with less competition and I guarantee you will become valuable again." I answered, letting the idiot know that I knew his current status.

Julie didn't bother to dispute my assumption. "How can I do that?" he wanted to know.
"By re-introducing him to me." I said. Julius called the Family. I knew the out-of-favor phony fairy was not even allowed to talk to Paulson directly, because I heard him say "please tell him right away, this opportunity might disappear fast."

## Chapter 52 Cows and Questions

Ten minutes later the phone rang and fifteen minute after that a black MB limousine rolled to a stop at the front door. We were invited to take a ride.

I was surprised to see Papa Paulson sitting in the back seat with two of his goons occupying the jump seats facing us.

"Where are we going?" Julius asked nervously.

Papa replied, "That all depends on whether or not you really can increase my profits and decrease my competition.
If you can we're going to my office, if not you are going to visit the countryside."

I spoke up in defense of the frightened little coward, "Julie did his part by bringing us together again. If you just passed out business cards I wouldn't have needed him any more than you do. It turns out you need the two of us. You need me to increase your bottom line; I need the fairy godmother here to help me decrease your competition. Now Papa do we go sight-seeing or do we pow-wow with scotch and cigars?"

Paulson nodded his head and one of the goons gave the driver instructions.

"It will be my pleasure Mr. Phantom to debate the state of the Families economy with you, while we are being entertained by Mr. Castro and Mr. Walker."

The limo took us back into town and deposited us in an elegant parking facility. Julie was ordered to wait in the lobby while we entered an elevator.

I was expecting to be taken to the penthouse, however adding to my perplexity the lift descended several levels.

The elevator doors opened to another door that responded to Papas fingerprints.

Once Mr. Paulson and I were ensconced in the very private Family Room I asked Papa to tell me what his most profitable business was.

I thought it was prostitution, and I just wanted verification before I explained how Andrew was already in the process of lowering the Family's competition.

Pete's immediate reply stunned me.

He said, "My casinos."

"Well," I confessed, "Papa, you just threw a monkey wrench in my plans. I was sure you banked most of your coin through the working girls.

Now you either give me a day or two to make revisions in my thinking or we take that ride to the country.

Do I call a cabbie or do you summon your killer coachmen?"

"If Julie was in this alone we would already have returned from cow country." The gang leader said "You, however, bring a different note to the song.

You came to me un-announced, convinced me of a lie, took what you wanted, and later secured your safety. Anyone that can do that to me deserves my attention.

You should know however, I was born with ADHD and its gotten worse. I have a very short attention span. This is Tuesday, if I don't hear from you by Saturday, with a workable solution to your proposition, I will probably forget all about this conversation and remember only that you promised me something you didn't deliver."

"Certainly little men who live in the south" Paulson opined, "will understand my consternation and tolerate any remedy I presumed compulsory."

The door opened and Papa's last remark was "see you Saturday?" Short Week.

The best thing that came out of that meeting was Papa Paulson's direct 'phone number. Now I'd better be able to use it before Saturday.

When Honey and Andrew were appraised of our current situation they were as surprised as I had been upon learning that it was roulette, not rouged and wet that brought Papa the mazumah.

We talked about other plans that would accomplish the promised results, and we found that changing gamblers habits is not as easy as changing rumpled bed sheets. We were making the easy change now with our current actions. There must be a way to implement the pussy-for-pay path to the developments we were seeking.

Taking brash actions was quickly becoming my way of life. I called Papa with the intention of convincing him to accept my original proposal of prostitution being the real road to greater profits.

A voice answered the ‘phone with “East side inflatable.”

I recognized the gang leaders voice. “Papa, the change we can make through gambling will work to fulfill the promise we made to you, but only for a very short time.”

Paulson’s interruption was music to my ears. “I’m glad you called; I was about to send out for you. I want you to leave my gamblers alone.

If it aint broke don’t fix it, and my poker games aint broke. My poker don’t need poked at. Capiche?

I breathed a sigh of relief.

“Yeah Papa I understand completely. What is your next largest earner?” Before he said anything I continued with “How do you feel about prostitution?”

For the first time, and I imagined for the last time, I would ever heard him laugh was when he said, “Now THAT you can fuck with!” he guffawed so hard I thought he was going to bust a gut.

I could just see it as he wiped tears from his eyes.

While still chuckling he said, "Well, it's not Saturday, you've got time to put it together."

Papa nicknamed me The Flash when I showed up at his office the next day with a plan that saved me from frolicking with the fishes.

I explained how Andy was taking the young whores off the street and helping them to stay straight, while I was doing the removal of the pimps.

Papa approved the plan that I created.

My part in my plan had to be postponed, possibly adjourned.

Catastrophe strikes in many, many ways. Tragedy came to me in a local 'phone call when my caller I.D. showed "Police Department".

I was afraid I was going to spend ten to twenty in a federal Hardship Hotel.

When the gendarme delivered the message it came as a much worse punishment than a simple conviction on any of the criminal deeds I had done.

My crimes could have resulted in the forfeiture of thirty, even forty, years of my life behind bars. But this!

The sentence was for life. I would have given my very soul, if only the words I heard were not true.

There was no need of an arrest, or of a trial, also there wasn't any use for a judge to formalize my conviction.

I was instantly incarcerated.

## Chapter 53 Old Is New

That horrible call was to tell me that my wife and my son were dead.

Later, Honey and Andrew both said I appeared to freeze, to become a statue.
Even today I wish they were right.
I wish that I was transformed into the effigy that my friends saw.
I still feel like a hollow image made of plaster, something easily broken and ground into dust.
Dust so finely milled the gentlest of breezes would blow me away.

I prayed for a hurricane to do just that, blow me into another dimension where I could undo what was done.

My wife and son did nothing wrong.
Nora and Matthew were just living their lives, expecting me home, for what they laughingly called one of my mini-vacations.

My family was returning home from a movie in Matt's Masarati when the fracturable sports car was T-boned by the drunken driver of a Ram 1500 4 wheeler.

I will never hold Nora in my arms again, or play piano duos with Matt. Tears come to my eyes and my heart aches from these memories that never leave my mind. My grief is so deep, so all pervasive, so wrapped around my heart and soul that I contemplated emulating the patrons of the Depot.

I seriously thought of taking heroin or coke or anything that would dull the terrible ache that made my living a travesty of life.

I wouldn't eat. I couldn't sleep. I was entirely inert in brain function until my body rebelled and I fell into a partial coma.

I awoke ravishingly hungry.

The forced sleep and tasteless food my body demanded gave me enough strength to begin to think again.

While still unwilling to face the world in person I needed to feed my mind as well as my body so I started to read. I read anything that was handy.

I read Nora's cookbooks, Matthews's books on Psychology, old newspapers.

I greedily consumed TV schedules, books of poetry, Psychology Today, Newsweek; I read anything and everything I could find.

It looked like my brain was starving too.

In one of the publications I found (I started to say 'I ran into' but I couldn't stand the picture that saying brought to mind so 'found' was the best I could do), I found something that ignited a small spark of recovery in me.

Perhaps it will help you in some way. This is it, a quote from George Henry Lewes quotes from BrainyQuote.com; "The only cure for grief is action."

My days spent in deep agony were not completely wasted.

It was during the suffering when I devised a way to do the only thing my heart kept beating for, to commit the perfect crime.

To get our revenge and do it in a way that no one knows but Nora, Matt, and me.

My mind wasn't as sharp as usual but the answer did present itself.
When I found the right person I would kill them with kindness.

No one has ever been convicted of being overly kind, have they?

I will soon know if G. H. Lewes spoke truth to my grief. I took action.

I went to the village where my family left me and started nosing around.

Some of the locals did as locals do when a stranger suddenly appears in their midst asking questions about death.

They got amnesia, couldn't remember a thing. That is, they couldn't remember anything except the Sheriffs telephone number.
I would say that it didn't take more than ninety minutes until I met the local Fuzz.

# Chapter 54 Coma

I introduced myself to Constable Roy Sparks as Private Detective Mark Phantom.
After producing the proper credentials and my badge I let the lawman know that I was in town to investigate a fatal accident. Sheriff Roy offered to contribute any accommodation that I needed.

Of course, my first requirement was for the police report of the deaths. Sheriff Sparks informed me that the report was not written by his officers but by the State Police Department. However Roy did produce a copy of the document and he did apologize for the lack of depth the report held.

The State Police report said only that a witness, Grant Bluewell, saw the Ram weaving down the road in front of his house.
Mr. Bluewell also said he saw the driver take a drink from what looked like a whisky bottle.
Other than a description of the wreck, that pretty much sums up the extent of the police report.

I did as the Phantom does and started from the end.
1. There was a devastating car wreck.
2. The Police report was skimpy. They knew only that it was a fatal hit-and-run.
No info on the second driver other than he was reported as a possible drunk.
3. The witness did not get the license plate

number.
The witness, Grant Bluewell, reported that it was not possible to get the plate number due to the way the vehicles crashed.
4. Nothing has been changed or added during the six months of my disability.

The police statement given by Mr. Bluewell, the witness to the accident, held an intriguing bit of information about why there were no license plate numbers gotten on the Ram 4 wheeler.

Grant said he didn't get the numbers because of the way the crash occurred.
This statement made me want to know how, exactly how, this wreck went down.

When I went to the hospital to talk to the E.R. about the accident I was told by the attending doctor that my family might have survived the wreck if the car hadn't turned over on top of them, crushing the sports car nearly flat.

At the time it didn't register with me that somewhere I heard that the Masarati sports cars were built so low to the ground that they should slide rather than tumble in most accidents.
I did remember that fact later.

I then decided my first stop should be with Mr. Bluewell to find out what he thought about the accident.

After I conferred with Grant Bluewell my grief was mixed with soul withering anger.
Bad enough that a drunken coward that left the

scene had decimated my family.
I found out why Grant didn't get the bastards plate number. My sons' car didn't tumble over on top of him and Nora.

That son-of-a-bitch in the 4 wheeler DROVE over them lifting the rear end of his truck too high to read the plate.

The heavy truck smashed the fragile car almost flat killing my beloved wife and son.

That unknown cocksucker murdered Nora and Matt.

I couldn't wait to get my hands on him, and I would put my hands on him.

In my conversation with Grant there was one little thing he remembered, but he thought it was too inconsequential to bother with.

Mr. Bluewell remembered catching a glimpse of the license plate as the truck zigzagged in front of his house.
The plate ended in x, which is all he could tell me. It wasn't much to go on, however it was enough to start with.

My first action on this shred of information was to look around at the trucks in the vicinity of the site where the murder took place. No luck.

To quote another philosopher;
Benjamin Disraeli once said;

"Action may not always bring happiness, but there is no happiness without action."
This too is from quotes from BrainyQuote.com.

The next move was to visit the local Bureau of Motor Vehicles. Out of luck again.

The B.M.V. said they had no authority to comply with my request for information without a court order.

Of course I didn't have a court order and would not get one without some form of evidence greater than an x, which I also didn't have.

Even if there is no happiness, still action was called for. Retribution may be at hand, and retribution may be all there ever can be for me.

I went directly to the state capitol where the B.M.V. is headquartered in the belief that under the right circumstances people will exceed any authority they may have for you.

Entering the building housing the offices that might be holding the information I was desperately in need of, I searched the directory that all large establishments displayed in their lobbies.

I chose an office on the thirty-fifth floor occupied by an official, Mrs. Longfield.

I have found that the higher you rise in a company, especially in government, the higher your office is located in the building.

Leaving the elevator I followed the signs to Mrs. Longfield's secretary's desk and introduced myself as Detective Mark Phantom.

## Chapter 55 Flattery Is A Tool

I could see the title disturbed the young man.

He asked me to wait, and then instead of using the intercom, chose to deliver the news of my arrival in person. Re-entering the reception room the young man held the door open and said "The Director will see you now Sir, please go in."

"Director" I said to myself, "better than I expected."

As I entered the well-appointed space an attractive, well dressed blond, stood. She asked,

"Detective Phantom how may we assist you?"

I replied, "I am investigating a murder case involving two vehicles and your help will be invaluable."

The Director said, "You flatter me Detective, but I'm afraid you came to the wrong department, this is the BMV not the FBI."

"No, Mrs. Longfield, I came to exactly the right place. I know that the department can't do anything for us, however I've been told," I lied, "that you have an understanding heart and a brilliant brain."

'We don't need more lawmen we need more information, more clues."

I paused to gage how my reply affected her.

I saw pleasure register in her eyes at the description of her heart and brain, then puzzlement as she heard the word lawmen.

I went on to describe the events of the car crash including how the hit-and-run driver deliberately ran his 4 x 4 over the small car, forcing the roof of the vehicle to smash the life from the occupants of the Masarati.
That callus action changed what happened from an accident into a murder.

Choking back my tears I continued by explaining that the only clue we had was that the truck was a 4x4 Ram with a license plate that ended in x.

I asked if there was any way she could help me without endangering her position.
In answer, the Director pushed a button on her desk.

Mrs. Longfield told her secretary she wanted an alphabetic listing of the owners of 4x4 Rams with a license plate that ended in x. She said she wanted the list by counties.
Mrs. Longfield also instructed him to have the list ready and on her desk in one hour.

After tasking the young man with this chore, she pushed a second button on the intercom.
A mans said "Yes Marcie? What's your problem?"
The Directors voice took on a sexy inclination when she said "You know damned well what my problem is Bob."

She assumed a more normal business-like tone. "I need a favor Commissioner. I need a complete report on every name in a list I am

sending over.
I want it a.s.a.p. And I want it on the down-low."

"Done, Director." He replied, "Suppose I have it delivered at breakfast?"

With a smile in her voice Mrs. Longfield said, "Thanks, Robert, breakfast sounds delightful."

Evidently Marcie remembered I was within the listening area.
"Bob and I are old friends," she said, "he's the Police Commissioner. He will be sending over enough work to keep you busy all weekend."

"That is the best I can do for you." she said, "You can have my list in an hour, if you care to wait, or you can pick up both lists tomorrow. They will be available by eleven tomorrow."

"I'll stay for the one you are getting ready now if you don't mind, so I can get started working right away."

I thanked her from the bottom of my heart for the immense help she was providing. "The FBI could not have done as well." I said.

Mrs. Longfield smiled as she said, "Flattery will get you anywhere, but you've already gotten as far as I can take you. The rest of this trip is up to you."

"Complements are not flattery when they are earned and when they are true." I said sincerely,

"Tell me of one other person in your Department of Justice you know who is capable of tying a clue like a single x on a license plate, to the need to narrow a search by looking through police records for possible DUI offenders?"

I continued, "And you're doing it so lightening fast."
The Director started to blush in an almost girlish manner, as color began to rise from her neck.

The bell saved Marcie when the door opened and her secretary came in with the work the Director wanted.

The B.M.V. finally provided me with a list of license plates ending in x.

I took the sheets of paper I obtained from the Director to my hotel room and began winnowing through the information, looking for anything that could point me to the murderer.

I started to wish I had stipulated the color red be included in the search criteria, but there was no concrete reason to do that. When Grant talked with me he did say that there was so much dirt stirred up that he thought the color was red, but he didn't really know for sure. Probably better to leave the color out.

I worked through the night and consumed gallons of black coffee along with two packages of Eagle cigarettes. I was reminded of stories my son told me about college life.

I made another pot of good-to-the-last-drop as I dove into a morass of facts and figures that at four o'clock in the morning still did not give up the information I needed. Possibly my quest would be more successful when the Commissioners list was added to the search. His list had complete information on each person who fit the criteria not just the bare facts I now had.

It is my opinion that the absolute strangest thing that exists in nature is the human brain. My personal mental computer may rank in the top one thousand of the weirdest such brains ever produced.

The reason for that belief is not complicated; it is, no matter what I know about anything, my brain commands that I do whatever sooths my heart and gut.

In my prevailing position my gut and heart overrode my brain again, and I labored through the long, difficult hours looking for any viable clue to the person who murdered my family.

It is seven thirty a.m. and still nothing solid shows up.

I shower and prepare for the days disclosures.

The B.M.V. receptionist must have been told I was expected. When I entered the building, she looked up and said “Good morning Mr. Phantom. The Director will be a few minutes late. She asked if you would care to wait in her office?”

When I was comfortably seated, watching the morning news, the male secretary brought me coffee and a scone. A quarter hour later Marcie showed up

"Sorry about the delay Mark, my breakfast with Bob ran over." She said with a smile.

I thanked her for her hospitality in providing something for my hunger while I awaited her arrival. The Director handed over the object that I really hungered for.

The item was a thumb drive that I hoped held the secret, for which I was seeking.

I was anxious to return to the hotel and to my laptop.

The lack of sleep and nourishment registered their presence on my body. I was starved, despite all of the coffee (ten cups), a few snacks, and the scone at the B.M.V.

I hadn't eaten a regular meal for fifty-two hours.

Sausage gravy and biscuits solved one problem. Six hours of slumber fixed the other.

I was now fit to work again and work I did. The thumb drive held hundreds of pages of large and small traffic offenses by Ram 4x4 truck drivers. I got my mojo back again. The Commissioner's list had more details, including the color of the trucks.

Thankfully I could arrange the reports by any or every category. Of course I started by the date of offense, then by the type offense, then by age of the driver, then by year of truck, then by the color. I'm sure I will re-arrange the categories several times before I'm satisfied.

Starting from the end as always, here is what we know:

1 Nora and Matt were murdered by a hit and run driver in a Ram 4x4 truck.

2 The driver may have been drunk.

3 The police report on the tragedy was bare.

4 There was one witness, Grant Bluewell.

5 The B.M.V. added some information to the paltry x that was the imperceptible clue we had to begin with.

This is what I found in the first twenty-four hours of my scrutiny.

By the offense: jail time. Almost all were simple teenage "under the influence" arrests.

By age: 18-50. The vast majority ticketed was between 18 and twenty-two.

By date of offense: the day I was told of the carnage, there were thirty-seven offenses. None involved damaged vehicles.

By year of truck: 2010. Out of thirty-seven there were five possible.

By color red: A very popular color. Four of the five trucks were suspect.

It looks like we have five to look at but it is really time to rearrange the data.

This time I wanted to know how many Ram 4x4s of any color or year were involved in an accident of any kind on the day my wife and son were murdered.

Now we see how any of the statistics captured in the first sorting were still in the second group.

# Chapter 56 A.A

The only absolute restriction placed on the searches was the date. This report expanded the possibilities from four or five to seventy-five.

Armed with some sustenance and sleep I took my suspicions to Grant Bluewell.
I asked Grant if there was anything he could think of that the police didn't ask him. He said he didn't think so.

When I asked him if the person he saw taking a swig from a whisky bottle look like a kid? Mr. Bluewell's memory got a little better. "No," was the emphatic response "I would have mentioned that whether or not they asked me.

I'm a twenty-eight year member of A.A. and I don't want any kid to get started walking in the gutter that booze put me in."

One more test and I was out of ideas.
I took three pens out of my pocket, a red, a blue and a green one. I put the pens on the table, and then asked Grant to watch a demonstration.

I left the green one on the table and taking the other two in hand I said, "Is this how you saw the accident happening?"

Not mentioning their color I said, "This one is the Masarati and this one is the Ram." Then I did a slightly askew t-bone with them.

"No" grant said, "the truck was in a straight line."

"Well" I said, standing and walking toward the door "that shows me I was right about how the truck could have run over them." I added nonchalantly " throw me that red pen on the table please." Grant looked at the pen, picked it up and threw it to me. "Thanks Grant."

Then holding up the green pen Mr. Bluewell had just tossed to me so it was in a well-lighted spot. I asked the eyewitness if this was the shade of red the truck looked like.
The aging man said he didn't get a good glimpse, but he thought so.

Grant Bluewell was not color blind.
Like so many people he saw colors. They were just wrong colors.

Speaking of things wrong, I began to think my approach to this problem might not be as right as I first thought.

In view of the fact that the only witness to this tragedy does not distinguish colors correctly, and our license plates are done in color, it is very possible that Mr. Bluewell did not see what he thought he saw. Now I am not at all convinced of my earlier belief.

All the same I don't intend to forsake my study of the information provided by Bob and

Marcie.

In any case I will also pursue a question I didn't ask anyone earlier. Because until now I was sure that I already knew the answer.

The puzzle becomes, why did the driver run the Masarati over?

Why? That is normally the second question my inquiring mind wants answered.

In my wildest conjecture there was no reason for the 4x4 driver to t-bone my sons car other than alcohol.

The driver of the 4x4 could have turned and stayed on the road, instead he went straight across Matt's car into a field.

Is another reason conceivable? Maybe.

In this special case my questions are like rabbits. The questions breed questions as fast as I can assimilate them.

Why drive into a field? Even a drunk knew that doing so would leave identifying tire marks, possibly paint chips on the foliage or other telltale signs of the murderers passing through the underbrush.

Why didn't the State Police report have anything on the truck except Bluewell's description?

From the case study it appears that the truck simply vanished. Why,why,why???

Ready or not I have no choice but to visit the scene of the crime again.

This time my brain was like a fox, sniffing out the trail the murderer must have left behind. This time my tears were gone so my eyes absorbed the field of corn stalks more clearly.

It was late August and the stalks still stood at attention in rows, as soldiers would have when guarding a farmer's now unproductive field.
There was no mention of any of those silent maze sentinels being destroyed by a 4x4.

Without question if the Ram had plowed into the corn stalks there would have been some sign of devastation. There was none. That observation brought on more questions.
Doesn't everything?

When was the field plowed and the corn planted? If it was in May, the month Nora and Matt were killed, I will be on the right track.

I must find the owner of the field to get this answer. It wasn't difficult to sniff out the proprietor of the acreage. I had only to ask the Sheriff who owned that tract of land.

Sheriff Sparks was quite familiar with the landlord, one Henry Lucas. They were cousins.
Mr. Lucas not only owned the farm I was interested in, he owned most of Mingo County.

The Sheriff told me his relative was an eighty-four year old gentleman who did not till the fields himself any more.

Mr. Lucas leased the lands. This particular plot was rented to a Donald Shrump.

The Lawman also said he couldn't figure out why his cousin kept leasing the farm to the ne'er-do-well. All the good-for-nothing did was drink for nine months and plant and reap corn for the other three while he was soaking up more booze.

This answer made Shrump a person of interest on the spot. I asked Sheriff Sparks if he knew where I could find Henrys tenant.

Sparks said it was dollars to donuts that Shrump was in the nearest bar.

I voiced the opinion that Sheriff Roy didn't care too much for Shrump as a farmer or as a man.

"Now what on earth gave you that idea? Just because I know there is something off about the jerk? Every day I look for a reason to run his finger prints so I could find out his secrets."

"Why not just take his prints from a glass and check them out?" I asked.

"Did you forget who you're talking to? I'm the Sheriff. That would be illegal." Sparks said. "Every citizen here knows I uphold the laws exactly as they are written, that's why these people trust me.

Keep that in mind the next time you jay-walk in this town." he ended with a laugh to lighten the gathering tension.

On my way back to the hotel a few of the rabbity questions were hopping back into their hutches. An answer or two was emerging.

Why was driving over the sports car into the field a good idea for whoever did it?

It was a particularly good idea if the furrows were in the same directions as the truck was traveling.

Because a plowed field, when planted, could hide information on the truck; especially hide things like the size and type, the tread design, and the manufacturer of the tires.

According to the standing stalks of corn they were all aligned in the direction the truck would have entered the field.

Who had knowledge of the way the rows ran in this cornfield?

The answer was, way too many.

Anyone that had seen the area before night fell on the day the wreck happened.

More people passed by this site during the day than attended an NFL championship game.

I can narrow the prospects down to one by adding the stipulation, how many do we know <u>without doubt</u> was aware of the condition of the field? The one person that did the work, the one that plowed the land.

Based on the following facts Donald is at the head of my list of the people who might have

murdered Nora and Matt:
Shrump owns a ram 4x4.
He is an alcoholic or at least a hard drinker.
He has knowledge of the plowed field.

I will be calling on Donald Shrump soon.

The question remains, why would such an extraordinary effort to protect the identification of the rubber? Another query is, does it matter?

I needed to get some R&R. The Rest was imperative. The Relaxation was impossible.

Settling for the doable I returned to my room and got a few hours of shut-eye.

The next morning I resumed my pursuit of the person responsible for the annihilation of my family.

First stop, the Sheriffs office.

"Good morning Sheriff, I'm here to turn myself in." I said cheerily.

"Good morning Mark" he replied, "What has the Phantom Agency gotten itself into?"

"My coffee tasted like crap this morning and I thought I'd like to kick the shit out of the guy that made my first cup of coffee of the day. It tasted like he brewed it using yesterday's grounds.

That morning cup is one of the few pleasures I have left."

"I can certainly sympathize with you" the Sheriff said "but I can't put you in jail for something I approve of, besides you didn't break any statutes.

# Chapter 57 Bar Hopping

"Shucks, Sheriff" I said in my best Mayberry accent, "I was taught that the thought is as good as the deed."

"Out of pure curiosity, Mark why do you want to be locked up?" asked the lawman.

"I want to meet your friend Donald Shrump." I answered. "From how you feel about him I figured he'd more or less be in permanent lockdown in your hoosegow."

"No, but I damn sure wish he was." came the quick reply.

"If not here, where?" I asked. "I don't want to spend all day every day looking in bars and other low dives for a face I've never seen."

"Spend some time in Town Tavern, his favorite honky-tonk.
Forget any concerns about his face; it's one of the ugliest mugs at any bar.

Red hair cut so short it's hard to tell the color, an often broken nose like a prizefighter might have, and eyes that never look you in the face.

Not only will you never forget what he looks like you will see him in your most ungodly nightmares. At least I do."

The Sheriffs words implied another mystery that might need examining, but I don't want to stay for another puzzle or to take too much on my plate right now.

I have other fish to fry and the skillet hasn't even gotten hot yet. There will be time for me to cast my net into the waters of wonder; if I am so inclined, after my creel is filled with the body of the killer I want to find.

Now it is time to fish the lake of liquor Roy had suggested.

I entered the lower middle class establishment Sheriff Sparks recommended.

These places were thinly attended so early in the day. There were always a few people seeking solace from one thing or another that is bringing them the kind of pain they're unable to handle in less self-destructive ways.

There is usually an additional one or two truly addicted sots, dedicated to destroying their lives through the medium of alcohol.

The Town Tavern was no departure from the norm.

In fact it was below par with only one patron imbibing at this early hour.

A male guzzler occupied the center stool. I took the seat to his left.

If any stranger ever sat beside me in a place with at least thirty other empty places to choose from, I would have been a little curious, suspicious even.

However this guy never even checked me out in the mirror backing the bar.

I didn't make any move of any kind toward him. We just sat. Each of us encased in his own private space.

The solitude was shattered when the bartender, a very attractive young lady, stopped filing her fingernails long enough to take my order.

"What can I do for you handsome?" she asked with a wink. That was either her standard opening designed to multiply whatever tip she might receive, or she was a part time hooker.

"Two doubles straight up, of the swill the drunk beside me is in to" I answered.

Curiosity couldn't cut the silence but Canadian Club straight up instantly straightened up my bar partner.

"Are both of those doubles for you?" is the first thing the pugilistic looking drinker sitting there said to me.

Don't be surprised, that he started that way, without any preamble. I wasn't.

One of the things Scruffy and company taught me was that addicts never think of anything except their addiction.
It comes before anything else in life.

Now the reason I wanted to get next to Shrump got into gear.

"No, they're not" I said, "presuming you are Donald Shrump."

"Sure I'm Shrump. What the fuck," Donald said "I'll be Santa Clause if it'll get me that CC. Why are you after him?" he said, reaching for one of the doubles. I stopped him, grabbing his wrist and slamming his hand on the bar.

"Didn't mama tell you curiosity killed the cat?" I said.

Donald did what I was hoping he would do. He fought back. He raised that very strong farmers hand I just slammed into the bar, and grabbed my forearm.

"Listen to me you son of a bitch" Shrump said as he jerked my arm so hard my head hit the padded armrest edging the mahogany wood of the bar.

"Didn't your mama tell you, cats have nine lives? If you want to keep the one life you have now you better tell me what you want from me; and if you ever grab me again you better pray to god he that he made you a cat."

If that padding hadn't been in place I would have been out cold. As it was my head was swimming, and my ears were ringing. Still I understood every word Shrump spit out.

"I want to have a drink with you" I said "and get to know you."

"Why?" he snapped. "Why do you want to be friends with me?"

"Who said anything about friends?" I asked, "I only want to know why Sparks hates you as much as he hates me." The bait is cast. Will the sucker rise to it?

## Chapter 58 Fishing the Alcohol River

"Sparks hates you too?" Shrump replied with a tinge of disbelief in his voice, "Why?"

"Are you ready to drink and talk some?" was my first tug on the line.

"If you make it big drinks and small talk you've got my attention."

The rod bent, the little bell tinkled, Donald took the worm, hook, line and sinker.

Now to reel the sucker in slowly so I don't loose my catch.

I said, "I'll spring for the sauce this time." "Do we go to your place or mine? I've got a great suite at the Marriott."

"Your place if we're drinking top shelf and using their room service." he said.

"Do you think Johnnie Walker Blue is top shelf?" I asked. "That's what I ordered last from the Marriott bar. I think there may be a few shots left in the bottle."

"Damn" he said, "one more double C here then we go to your place."

Shrump threw his double down, coughed once, seized my arm and we headed for the door.

You might be confused by my largesse; so let me take a moment to explain my generosity.

One of the things, conceivably the only thing, that Grant Bluewell, was sure about was that the driver of the 4x4 was drinking.

I am convinced a recovering alcoholic like Grant would see that if he saw nothing else.

This, coupled with the Sheriff's information about his cousins tenant, and the overall attitude of this barfly makes me think I may be close on the trail of the object of my revenge.

I need to be positive of my prey, because I am also convinced that you know my revenge is the forfeiture of the killer's life.

My generosity is simply an investigative technique.

The Donald was so anxious to get to the Johnnie Walker that he didn't notice that my double C.C. was untouched. We got to my hotel in record time.

And now I'll firmly set the hook and bring this fish to the frying pan.

Drunks love to confess their sins for some reason. If Shrump did reach the tell-all point I would either send him home, or send him to hell, depending on what he confessed.

It took Donald a lot of drink to reach that stage.

I saw to it that he got all he needed.

Before the night was over I wanted to know if I would learn absolutely if this pitiful person was the driver of the murder weapon.

If what Shrump spilled didn't qualify him for Hades or home then I would give him to Sheriff Sparks.

Late in our heart-to-heart I got us started bragging about the possible military use of our trucks.

I said my 150 would carry more men and ammunition up to the front lines than the Ram could, and my truck could do it faster, even with a heavier load. Donald scoffed and said his Ram can take a harder hit because of its thicker body.

I laughed at him, which really pissed him off.

"A Ram my gazoo!" I said, "That motorized piece of crap would be better named Ewe, as in Phew!"

I told Shrump the enemy could drive their vehicles right up his ass, and make all his soldiers prisoners, while they took all of his ammunition to use against us.

I could see Shrump really was getting angrier and angrier the longer we argued.

He was also getting drunker and drunker.

Then I tried to make it worse when I said the whole undercarriage of his Mickey-mouse truck would fall off, as soon as the Ram hit a big bump.

Shrump, now three sheets to the wind, shouted "That's a damn lie, my Ram is a fuckin' tank. My 4x4 would flatten their dammed motorcycles, cars, trucks, or any fuckin' thing else they've got. It can just run over any fuckin' thing the enemy has."

"Bull shit" I shouted back "that kiddy-car can't hardly get over a curb.

When did that overpriced piece of 4 x shit ever run over anything bigger than your girlfriends tits?"

That exchange, and enough liquor to take a bath in, was enough to let his tongue override his brain.

"Not too long ago" he blurted out "some shit head in a foreign car pulled out in front of me and I t-boned the fucker!

I just kept going like he was only a little speed bump in the road.

When has your mammy jammin' truck done anything like that?" he ended his taunt with a smirky, "Huh? When asshole? Tell me when or pour me another Blue."

"Keeping my rage in check I smiled and said. "You win Donald. I could never do that. You deserve another double.

In fact I'll call room service and order two more bottles."

Shrump slurred, "Terrific" as he slopped scotch on his face trying to down the drink I poured for him.

I made the room service order, telling the clerk my friend wanted two bottles to take home with him.

This is the final gift that I, or anyone, will ever give to Donald Shrump.

In short, I am going to murder the murderer.

If you have been keeping up with the adventures of the Phantom Agency you are aware of my occasional need to maim or even to kill in the line of work.

These deaths were in every case justified homicide in order to protect society at large.

My taking of life in this instance will be outright murder to try to cure my abiding grief.

This may or may not be the kind of action Lewes was talking about but it is the malicious action my bleeding soul cries out for.

I consider it entirely justified.

I'm going to give Donald Shrump what he considers the perfect gift. I gave him three bottles of Johnnie Walker Blue. Very kind of me, wouldn't you say? The hotel clerk thought so. Danny said he'd put the booze in a hotel gift bag for me.

Then, before we called it a night, I saw to it that Shrump drank enough of the excellent scotch to cause alcoholic poisoning.

## Chapter 59 Feeding The Fish

Thirty-to-forty minutes from the time room service delivered the gift bag I made absolutely certain Donald choked down four eight ounce glasses of Blue. After consuming such a large amount of booze, more than sufficient to cause his death, the Donald will pass out. Forever.

Once the lethal dose is ingested it takes a little while for the victim to expire.

There was time enough for the desk clerk to see me helping Shrump stagger out of the door with the hotel goody bag under his arm.

As I returned to my room the clerk and I said our goodnights to each other.

I got comfortable on the bed with a cup of hot black coffee and turned on the scanner Phantom uses to track police activity when we needed to.

Tonight we needed to.

The radio crackled in about twenty minutes and a patrolman reported finding a dead man lying in enough vomited up blood to fill a tub.
The corpse was found cradling the bag full of empty scotch bottles that I sent Shrump home with.

I got my first good nights sleep since Shrump ran over the Masarati and murdered my family.

I called Sheriff Sparks the next morning to tell him I had some news for him. Of course the Sheriff said he had some news for me too.

Sparks wanted to know if I knew anything about Shrump, since I was seen drinking with him.

I said, "I sure do, I know he's a rotten bastard." I told Roy that I was interrogating Donald to find out if he knew anything about my case. I said Shrump demanded to be paid in hootch for what he knew.

I had to pay him only to learn that he was as dumb as a box of rocks. It was a total waste of good scotch.

The asshole didn't know a damn thing except how to get drunk.

I also told the Sheriff he was right about Shrump. I did get something else out of him.

Donald was a no-gooder; Shrump admitted to me that he was stealing tires from the Goodyear plant. So the Sheriff's wish can come true, he could pick up the drunk and throw Shrump under the jail if you want to.

Roy sounded disappointed when he told me, "It's too damned late. Donald Shrump is dead."

"What happened?" I asked, and then I said, "He was O.K. when he went home this morning. Drunk and sleepy but alive and walking."

"I know", Sparks, replied, "I checked with Danny, the night clerk. He told me he saw Shrump leave and that he was drunk but O.K. Danny told me that Donald left alone and you went back to your room and didn't leave again."

# Chapter 60 Jiggery Jig

I said, "Sorry that he died," I lied, "what happened to him".

"He drank himself to death. It's just as well," Sparks, said, "it had to happen sooner later."

We said our goodbyes and I left town only return home to an empty house.

There were thirty calls on the Phantom answering machine. Some of the calls were repeats, some were of no interest, a couple might be worthy of callbacks, and one demanded my attention.

That was an international call from Manny Guzmahn.

I fixed some frozen waffles, got a cup of coffee and mulled over the South American call.

While dinking my fourth cup of Folgers I decided not to put off the inevitable any longer and placed the call.

All I knew of Guzmahn came from Honey and Andrew, that Little Man was aware of me at all must have also come from the Devil & Angel pair.

Guzmahn and I had never met. I called the callback number the drug lord used when he left the message on my answering machine.

Mannys' greeting was an example of why he was admired by his men, even loved by many of them.

This is how he answered his ‘phone. “Mr. Phantom, thank you for getting back to me. Please know that I offer you my sincere regrets on the loss of Nora and Matthew, and my congratulations for your successful punishment of the perpetrator of their demise.”

Needless to say his words made me take a few moments to reply.

“Thank you Mr. Guzmahn,” I said, “for your expression of sympathy, I appreciate it. How did you know I earned your congratulations?”

“Mr. Phantom,” Little Man replied, “you returned my call, which means you got my message. That means you returned home. That is an action you could never tolerate with such important business left unfinished.”

I complimented him on his excellent use of logic and asked him to call me Mark. Guzmahn agreed and said I should call him Manny.

“Fine Manny.” I agreed, “ Now what was the purpose of your call? It wasn’t exclusively to express your condolences I’m sure.”

“No, not exclusively,” Manny confessed, “Although that was an important reason for me to call a friend of my friends. The other reason I called is best discussed in person. May I send a plane for you? I want to retain your services.”

There was no reason for me to stay in town right now.

This is a perfect opportunity to escape a house that was no longer a home, so I agreed.

"Wonderful," Manny said, "there will be a car for you in ten minutes. We can discuss business over dinner this evening."

I have always admired decisive people.

I was in Little Man's compound in time to wash up before the meal. After we ate we talked. "I am having a problem with a party breaking their promise to some very important associates of mine." Guzman said,

"I could end the problem myself but that might cause ripples. I want to be incognito in this affair with no possible string connecting me."

"O.K." I said, "It's time I went back to work. Give me the who, what, and when."

Manny said, "You know the actors in this play. You even know the contract that was broken. There's a good chance you know how I want the curtain to come down."

I replied "That's a start, now fill me in on the cast."

I was flabbergasted by the unbelievable response. Little Man said, "They are, Andy, Honey, Papa, you and me."

"Now that you know the cast," Little Man said. "Let me fill you in on the plot."

"I wish you would," I said. "Although I am technically already on retainer for some of the characters and I will not engage in any conflict of interest, not even for you."

"Thank you," Manny said, "I'm going to sketch out a few things and you can make your decision whether or not to take the case. O.K.?"

I saw the smile on his face and I thought this might be exactly my cup of tea so my answer was, "I would absolutely be interested in getting to the meat and potatoes, on my terms."

The smile broadened as Guzmahn said, "You are the reason I am involved in this at all." "You used my name, without my permission by the way, to bargain with a local gangster.

In fact, you threatened him with my deadly retaliation in the event that this crook didn't comply with your request."

Little Man explained. "Normally I'd send one of my men to visit anyone with the audacity to do what you did."

I asked, "Then why was I spared the sweet sleep your assassins specialize in?"

The answer he gave showed me a glimpse of the drug lord few people saw.

"Because, Mark, or Charles, which was the name you used with Papa Paulson, you performed your perfidy to save a very good friend of mine, to whom I am deeply indebted.

I believe Andrew Smyth is also a good friend of yours. Nevertheless, your action resulted, as do so many things, in unintended consequences."

"Like putting you in a position where you must do battle with one of your own kind?" I asked.

"No, no," he said, "this small time punk is not of my own kind, but he is one of my clients, and the cartel frowns on knocking off it's paying customers."

I wore a puzzled look when I said, "If this is simply a matter of killing someone, you already have that kind of drudgery covered with your own people.

You don't need me for blood work."

"In the cozy confines of the Devil & Angel, Honey and Andy told me tales about a man named Manny." I said. "The person they spoke of to me would never do harm to his friends either. Quite the contrary, this man would do as I will do and act <u>for</u> them."

I added, "You spoke of Andrew as a friend. My assumption is that Honey is also privileged to be in that category?"

"Naturally," he said.

"I too think of them as my friends." I said. "I will <u>not</u> act against them.

If you think our friends are responsible for breaking some sort of promise to you, and you want to hire me to straighten them out, this confab is over, you are no longer the man my friends admired, and I am leaving." I said as I arose.

"No need for a hasty exit." my aspiring employer said, "I will never raise a hand against Andy or Honey; Or against you now.

# Chapter 61 The Contract

To paraphrase an old saying, "The Friend of My Friend is My Friend."

Guzmahn looked me in the eye, and said, "If we fight it will be side-by-side, or back-to-back against our enemies. Never face to face against each other."

"That's a relief." I said "so let's stop feeling each other out then and get back to the assignment and to the reasons for it."

We made ourselves comfortable for the coming consultation, and a change started to come over the overlord. The hard featured face and fire pit eyes of a man without pity or compassion replaced those of my new friend. Little Man was in the house.

I honestly don't believe that Manny was aware that he was transforming into the man that was loved by many and feared by thousands.

"You promised Papa Paulson that we owed him one, because he not only released Andrew from captivity, but Mr. Paulson also agreed to let Smyth resign from The Family and continue his good work at the Devils & Angels without interference."

I hurriedly interjected "Little Man, that was just a parting phrase, it was like 'see you' or 'later' it wasn't meant to be taken literally."

That cold hard face turned those blistering eyes on me. When I was able to breath again I heard Little Man say, "Relax friend. It was not an accusation. I was merely reminding you of what was said. I know that Paulson knew it was not meant as a real promise."

I said, "As we were leaving Papa even said he owed us too. I knew it was just a way to say goodbye and didn't really mean anything."

Little Man asked, you do remember what they say about "unintended consequences"?" "How do you imagine a teen-age member of a neighborhood gang became the boss of a state-wide "Family'" of gangs at such an early age?"

It took a few seconds for me to answer. When I did speak I gave Little Man my considered opinion.

"Because Paulson is an intelligent, ruthless, insidious, traitorous, talented, gambler willing to lie, cheat, betray, or kill anyone, for any reason."

"You have nailed it on the head, yet you were willing to work with him. I don't need to ask you why you would do that, I know why. Phil Paulson has been my customer for a long time.

The first thing I learned about Papa was his ability to make people think he was in a position to do something they wanted done, without telling them why or how he could do it.

Papa lied. He occasionally came through, largely by accident. It was rare, but it was enough for the marks to believe his lies.

I also learned how to control the dog. Paulson has an enormous ego. Knowing that one single trait let me play Phil like a castanet. With a few kind words and phony compliments Mr. Paulson would betray anyone or anything, a cat, a confidant, or a country.

Tell Phil how brilliant you considered him to be and Papa pranced to the fiddler's tune, no matter what the fiddler fiddled or where the dances led.

That's why I kept Paulson out of power and isolated him from other members of the cartel.
I used Papa to open up my sales in areas where it was too dangerous for me to risk my boys getting killed. "Papa" on the other hand has no compulsion against sending his own "children" to a sure death, if in the end there is money or power in it for himself."

The fire in his eyes appeared to rise when this king of the cartel said "Now we come to why I want you for this job."

If you are ever caught in the glare of an internal inferno like the one behind Little Man's eyes I can tell you now that you will be inclined to do whatever the stoker says.

This fireman said "One of the reasons I can't step in, or even let it be known that I am involved, is that Paulson technically has broken no promise to me. For that matter he didn't break his word to you either. Phil has not bothered Andrew.

Papa is bothering Honey.
Paulson has her running mule again.

If she refuses to pack his dope Paulson promised to take her boyfriend out.

He also promised her that if Andy interferes Paulson will sick his sickos' on Honey.

This has been going on for a couple of weeks now. Phil is putting Honey in more and more precarious situations.

It's as if he wants her to get caught or killed, to make you suffer for out smarting him in Andrews's release.

With an ego as big as Paulson's you never forget a defeat.
I can shield Honey in this part of the world but it is much more difficult to keep her safe in other places.

We are watching the third act, Mark.
How will this drama conclude? With curtain calls or just with curtains?"

"Curtains." was my unequivocal answer, "This is definitely the last act. The last applause for Papa or for me.

One of us will be on stage taking a bow to the audience, the other one will be on the Road of Good Intentions taking a trip to the afterlife."

We agreed I needed to formulate my future actions and that time was of the essence.
Little Man's informants told him Honey was scheduled for another run in four days.
Coffee cups clicked in a toast as these two friends vowed not to loose their other two friends.

I was flying home an hour later. I needed to get back to work.

Now you will see the difference in a leader and a tyrant demonstrated. Remember how Manny greeted me on my return from near necrosis?

This was the greeting I received when I walked into Phillip “Papa” Paulson’s office.

“Phantom! Good to see you.
I’ve been waiting for you to get back to work. I can’t rest ‘til you get rid of certain pimps that have been trying to recruit in my territory.”

Not a word of comfort or concern for me on my return. It was all about Papa and his needs.

Is it any wonder that leaders are respected and tyrants are hated?

The way I smiled and the cheerful answer I gave masked my true feeling that I wanted to choke the bastard to death.

Killing Phillip “Papa” Paulson strikes me as being a piece of cake.

I wonder why no one has chopped off his noggin so far?

Maybe I’m the only one Paulson trusts enough to get this close to him.
The thought of getting to turn his lights off because I am so trusted is a real downer.

It means that I am more like Papa than makes me comfortable.

# Chapter 62 To Kill A Killer

Then the rock of reason crashed through the window of my memory, with the name Potter written on it in blood.
Logic re-entered my brain and the thought of the disposal of the gang boss was no longer a problem for me. The immediate problem now was how to get away with murder. Again.

I devised a plan that would solve Peter's problem, and help keep Honey safe at the same time.

Papa is not an addict, he just sells addictive shit. He is not a gambler, he just takes the house rake. Phil is not a lush, so I can't make him commit suicide by booze as I did with Shrump.

Time is short, and so it would seem, is my imagination

How the hell can I dust him and come away clean? The plan is simple; kill the man threatening Honey and Andy. The way to execute the plan is not so clear.

The clock was reading near midnight and Mr. Coffee was calling me. I swallowed half a cup of hot Maxwell House.

Then the mallet struck the midnight gong and jarred a great memory loose in my cranial synapse. I knew how to get to Paulson!

Little Man told me Papas weakness.
It was Phillips enormous chutzpah.

All I require now is a challenge that Paulson will accept; even knowing that if he fails it could be self-destructive.

A public challenge to him that his enormous self esteem wont let him refuse would be best.

A challenge guaranteed to beat him.

What does Paulson enjoy doing? Sports? Baseball? Football? Soccer? Tennis? Golf? Skeet shooting? Archery? Hunting?

The only thing I know Papa is good at is short-range annihilation by pistol.

How am I going to discover his fondest wish in time to figure out how to use what I don't know against him?

I do know the simplest way to gain any sort of information is to ask for it.

How can I ask Paulson how to kill him in a way that doesn't tip my hand?

As usual in my investigations there is a point at which I have no fuckin' clue how to progress.

This is the spot where I rely on luck to lead me. I made an appointment with Papa through his always-open office, for eleven this morning then I laid down for a power hour of sleep.

Hot coffee and pastries were on the sideboard in Paulson's office when I got to the meeting.

"Good morning Papa. Let me start with the bad news. I found out last night that Honey is not available to work our plan on a regular basis. She is otherwise engaged part-time doing something or other for someone else.

I thought you should know why things are not happening as fast as we had hoped. Honey will still help out, but this development will slow down our schedule considerably."

"Not to worry, Flash. I know all about it." Paulson said.

"You do?" I responded, sounding surprised. "Yeah I do" he continued " you see when you told Honey I was helping out the cause, she volunteered to run some errands for me from time to time as her way of saying Thanks. I accepted.

That's all there is to it. The slow down won't be that bad."

"I wonder why Andy didn't tell me she was helping you?" I said. "I guess it doesn't matter." I said dismissively, "It's a relief to find we're all on the same page."

As Papa and I talked about his competition and the places he was most interested in controlling, we were distracted by a number of Family underlings asking for instructions.

Papa ran a very tight ship so interruptions such as these didn't bother him and they gave me a perfect path to my end.

"Man! I can almost cut the tension around here with a switchblade." I spoke with a smile, and continued with a very loaded question embedded in my statement.

"I'm going to take tomorrow off and just do something to relax. You know, "All work and no play makes Jack a dull boy". Hey Papa, why don't you come with me? All we do together is work. I'll bet we would have a hell of a good time socially." This is where I learn once again if the Lady is still with me.

Paulson has no friends. I think no one has ever asked him to do any fun thing.

At least that is one of my critical suppositions.

Even those among us that barely qualify as human want a piece of the friendship action.

That demand of our DNA for fidelity prompted Papa to agree to go with me.

Luck <u>was</u> a Lady today.

All the same, the inherited stitch in Paulson's psyche called for caution. Thus Papa's question, "Go with you where and do what?"

"What difference does it make? We can both afford to go anywhere and do anything." I said, "Isn't there something you have long desired to do? Some place you would love to visit?"

## Chapter 63 Take A Trip

Not a milli second later I had the answer to his dreams and to my problem. Or did I have another problem?

"Greece." The word fairly jumped from his mouth and Paulson went on with a faraway look in his eyes, "I want to walk through the once beautiful temple of Athena.
I want to run the route of the original marathon.
I want to Sail and fish the Aegean Sea, and I want to go to the Isle of Lesbos to see where my sisters lovers sprang forth."

"Damn, Papa that will take more than a day. More like a month. Maybe a month of Sundays." I said.

"You wanted to know what I wanted to do. These are all in my bucket list," he said rather wistfully.

"Then I'm in!" I said with a big grin, "We leave for Greece in the morning."

My enthusiastic accord brought Paulson a huge grin on a face that nearly never cracked a smile.

That pleasant countenance remained in Paulson's features even after I said, "Oh, wait. I have to take some time trying to find someone to fill Honey's absence from the Devils & Angels. This chore may take a day or two. You must have some things to settle too, but we'll leave on the first flight we can manage."

"No!" was the emphatic but still cheerful objection from Paulson. "I'll tell Honey she can take some time off from my errands. She can go back to helping Andrew until we return. I'll leave my business in the hands of my second in command.

Does that satisfy your prerequisite? If so we fly out in the morning. Who knows he said, we leave tomorrow, maybe never to return!"

I said yes and Phillip Papa Paulson had his assistant book the flight for Athens on a journey to empty his bucket list. We flew Aegean Air to Spata.

We checked in to Sofitel Athens Airport hotel, and then we left immediately for the Parthenon and the Temple of Athena.

I was dumbfounded when I stood by as Papa prayed at the spot where the great statue of Athena once stood. This was a Paulson I never dreamed existed.

To my wonder it was this Praying Papa I never dreamed of that suggested the way to fill my absence from the Devils & Angels.

Dumb was the operating part of how I felt. You will learn why later.

The Isle of Lesbos was next on our agenda. Paulson was so taken by the Parthenon that we stayed late and the Isle was rescheduled for the next day.

I considered that to be a lucky break because I had not yet figured out how to discharge my obligation to Little Man.

After a long day and an excellent dinner of Lamb Kleftiko we discussed the day's events. We also talked about my method of increasing the bottom line for his businesses back home.

"I know Andrew can use all the help he could get." So saying, Paulson picked up his telephone and called his second in command. "Hank" papa said "I want Honey released entirely from her work for me. Tell her to go back to Andy and help him do what they do. Tell our boys on the street to see to it that she and Andrew Smyth are <u>not</u> interfered with. You got it? Get someone else to run the errands. Yes, now.

Hell no we're not going out of business. Not yet anyway. You keep things cool 'til I get back. I don't know." Papa disconnected.

Now you know why the Praying Papa dumbfounded me.

My brain thought my ears were on somebody else's head. What the hell, I must have fallen asleep and I'm dreaming all this.

It was not possible Paulson was saying what I was hearing.

This feared killer, Papa Paulson, would never say what these ears are listening to; but these human headphones heard it in stereo.

## Chapter 64 Sightseers

"Hank wanted to know when I was coming back," Phil said "I told him I didn't know."

Then another little firecracker went off. "If you want too" he said, "we can stay a month. Hell, I think I could stay here forever."

This guy has gone nuts I thought.

That is exactly what Guzmahn wants, I said to myself, for you to stay here forever, and it is my job to see to it that you do.

The situation has changed since we came to Greece. Phil is exhibiting signs of virtuousness.

Do old instructions still apply?

Papa Paulson released Honey from the clutches of The Family permanently.

Papa said a prayer, perhaps to the wrong god, but that shows he is capable of piety.

Phillip is displaying true friendliness in our relationship. That in its self was a shock to my system.

That last feature is beginning to irk me because Papa is still scheduled to become part of the Grecian firmament. That part was up to me, and I don't relish the thought of offing what is now a friendly acquaintance.

For all of his apparent reformation however, Paulson was still the man that had planned on killing my friends.

Detaining him in this ancient land was apparently slowing down that murderous process, but was it changing the plan?

Like it or not, I still held his contract. Perhaps today I will be inspired when we visit the home of Sappho.

I did think there might have been a chance to end the threat to Honey and Andy when we went to see the petrified plants at Polichnitos on the Isle of Lesbos.

However I tried in vain to find a way to make Paulson "accidentally" stumble and fall and impale himself on a petrified tree stump.

Furthermore my job for Guzmahn was becoming an uncomfortable obsession.

I was troubled because Greece seems to have worked a very good transformation in Paulson. There no longer seemed to be any threat to our friends

We only left home a short time ago so it's too soon to be sure there is going to be a profound change in Phillip, but my gut says there is, and my gut is rarely wrong.

Therefore there no longer seemed to be any reason to eliminate Phil. I'll check with Manny.

I must be obsessive. I continuously think of ways to off Paulson as soon as I wake up 'till I go to sleep. Why else do I keep on that course when I doubt the validity of the mission, and when every plan fails?

If repeating the same action over and over and expecting a different result is the definition of insanity; then continuing to hold on to a plan, when you really don't want the plan to work, must be the definition of obsesseiveness.

I have to call Guzmahn soon.

Our retracing the route of the marathon may bring clarity to my present dilemma.

To Panathenaic is a long way to run. So we didn't run. We started to trot, then to walk fast, and finally to walk at a stroll.

It took us a lot longer than 2 hours 50 minutes and 58 seconds, the time it took Spyridon Louis to win the first Olympic Marathon.

The more time we spent walking together, the more Papa and I talked. We discussed many things. These topics included his many legal and illegal activities.

It also included a confession. Papa let me know of his intention, which he has abandoned, to have Honey either arrested, or eliminated permanently just to get back at me for having bested him.

Paulson told me that he really didn't understand the rationale, but he has begun to have misgivings about all of the criminal facets of his life.

"It must be the fact that this excursion with a friend

has opened my eyes to how much more there is to living." There it was, the friend word again.

"It doesn't hurt to know that my double entry bookkeepers have informed me that my personal income is higher from the legit side of the ledgers since that was all in my name and was never split with The Family."

Peter laughed and gave his "friend", me, a slap on the back and said, "You never woulda thunk it, huh? Me too."

There you go again, I thought, throwing around the friend word. I'm calling Guzmahn tonight.

We hailed a cab to take us back to the Grande Bretagne.

After we showered and relaxed with a little coffee and Grand Marnier we dined on Moussaka and Ouzo, then continued with the strong coffee and orange brandy.

We reached the "tell all of your secrets" point of our intoxication when Papa dropped another Bunker Buster on me.

"You know, Mark," he said with a crooked grin, "there is another small scheme I've decided to scrap?"

"No" I answered, "now what is bouncing around in that evil brain?"

"I was going to do <u>you</u> in while we on this trip, but you really did become my friend.
I never had a friend before, not even as a kid. I like you, so I am swallowing my considerable pride, and forgetting that you conned me."

Papa continued with, "Not only will I not do you in, I'll protect you from now on.

That's what friends do, no? I just hope you like me too and won't scam me again."

"How about that for letting it all hang out?" He laughed and reached for the Grand Marnier.

"Thanks, Phil." I joined in his mirth and said, "I may need your protection."

With that said we drank in silence 'till we turned in.

I got up early and dialed Manny. Little Man's private number rang nine times before he answered with a surly voice, "Yes. Who is this?"

The voice was a touch less combative when I told him who it was, and that I was calling from Greece.
Nevertheless it was definitely not Manny I was talking to. It was Little Man.

I asked, "What's wrong?"

His reply was less than encouraging.
I must have picked the worst possible time to try to get any kind of a concession from Guzmahn.

These were his words, "Are you calling to I tell me Papas' gone? If not, why not?"

"No, Little Man," I said, "He is still with us. That's why I'm calling."
Needless to say this was not the best time for me to talk about him. "Why are you so on fire?"

"I am upset because last night we got a lot of shit from Paulson's camp.

It's taken care of now, but how in hell did he cause so much trouble while he's not even in the country? And with you watching him? You <u>are</u> watching him?"

"Certainly, Little Man. Phil is never out of my sight except when we are sleeping. Then <u>I</u> have his 'phone.

When Papa makes calls during the day I'm always listening. His calls are what I want to talk to you about when you settle down."

Controlled anger conspicuous in his voice, Little Man said, "Settle down my ass. Settle accounts is more like it."

I said, "There are things happening here that might change your mind. It's difficult for me to explain them on the 'phone when you're pissed."

Little Man said, "Give it your best shot. The worst is over here. We got rid of Papa's right hand man, Hank, last night, so there's nothing pressing me at the moment. What do you want to say?"

"We are in Greece. We're a long way from home. It would be awful hard for Phil to direct any kind of disturbance against you from here.
I know Paulson gave Hank an order to keep things cool 'till we return. There's more we can talk about when I come home.

In the meantime, Little Man, here is something you might want to pay attention to.

Aristotle, a famous son of the Greeks once taught this."

"Anybody can become angry — that is easy, but to be angry with the right person and to the right degree and at the right time and for the right purpose, and in the right way — that is not within everybody's power and is not easy."

"I know you have the power to do hard things Little Man.

I continued speaking to the Master of Mayhem with all I had left by giving him that sincere compliment; followed by advice to a multi trillionaire, the world's largest drug dealer.

Sleep on these ancient, but appropriate words of Aristotle, Manny and I'll call again tomorrow." I said goodbye and hung up.

Tomorrow, I thought, is another day.
I never did figure out why something so obvious was supposed to be a saying so full of wisdom. There is no guarantee of a tomorrow for any of us.

There is less than none for me and for the company I kept.

Still and all, despite my pessimism God turns on the sun and we are allowed to see the virtue, and the sin, in our world and in our hearts one more time every morning.

Speaking of the sunrise reminded me that it was time to finish emptying Paulson's bucket list. Today we go fishing on the Aegean.

We didn't find a commercial fishing boat for rental soon enough to satisfy Phil, so he bought a vessel and hired a captain who knew these waters to take us out.

We decided not to cast off until early the next morning to give the captain time to outfit our craft properly. I wouldn't have time to call Little Man tomorrow until we returned.

In the meantime we explored the ouzeries of Greece and we tried to learn a few words of the language.

As we sipped from a bottle of ouzo, Phil and I learned why Greek men are so famous for their love of conversation. The licorice flavored drink tends to loosen your tongue. At least it did for us.

I told Papa about my 'phone call to Little Man. Including the fact that his second in command was dead. I also told Phil why Hank was killed.

## Chapter 65 Small Fish In a Big Pond

Papa was visibly upset. "Hank was my cousin," he said, "I told the idiot to keep things cool until we returned.

He always wanted to be boss, so he made his move to take over while I was here in Greece and couldn't fight back. Hank always was a coward. That's why he never could be number one."

"I'm sorry." I said.

"Don't be," Papa said, "I'm not. This event is going to set me free, and make you a hero."

"Hero?" I asked, "How can a trip to Greece and the death of your cousin set you loose and make me heroic?"

"Easy, you tell Little Man that I am getting out of the rackets and that he can have one of his lieutenants take over everything in the morning."

A skeptical enquiry popped out of my mouth "For what in return?"

My friend Phil chuckled as he answered my question.

"For a sign of good intentions, as a white flag, or a good deed. Maybe as a parting gift from a multi-millionaire tired of watching his back, to a many times over trillionaire.

I don't think Little Man will look this gift horse in the mouth."

I made the call to Guzmahn with the news of the good deed Phil did for him, and suggested that he cancel the contract, which he did. More good news was the considerable bonus Manny sent to my bank account.

There's an old saying that no good deed goes unpunished. Phil did his good deed for Little Man last night. The universe dished out the punishment in short order. We were on the yawl early the next day doing what Phil had dreamed of doing for many years. We were sailing and fishing the Aegean.

Captain Alex did know these waters well. We caught our first fish a half-mile off shore.

The catch called for a celebration. As we lifted our bottles to toast our fishing prowess, a strong gust of wind tilted our craft just enough to throw Papa Paulson overboard.

The last Alex and I saw of my new friend, the newly reformed gangster leader, he was sinking under the Aegean Sea. We tried to fish Papa out of the water and onto the boat, but we couldn't find him. Phil was gone.

Little Man's order was satisfied. The Universe did the job I had decided not to do.

I have lost too much. Nora, Matthew, and now my new friend, Phil are all gone. I need a long vacation.

I called Honey and Andy and told them I was taking a hiatus, but I would come back, someday.

Maybe I'll tackle the jobs I put off 'till later when I come back. Right now I'm going to tour the Mediterranean.

Perhaps you and I will meet again when I return. "Until then, stay well my friend."

Mark Flanagan
The Man That Loves You,